PROLOG

The thoughts and writings of gods and monsters have long been involved in the history of human kind with a great deal of Biblical history being proven by science on almost a daily basis. In as much as the Bible is being proven, Greek, Egyptian and other mythologies are also finding credence in the scope of possible alien foundations or might those be of angels and demons? I am not one to dismiss any of it as, in my opinion, the writing of the Bible has been perverted by men that wanted to use it to control the masses. Much of it has been destroyed and much is finally coming to light as fact. While the Bible is being proven, the myths and legends of previous civilizations are considered to be false without any real examination. But so much of our stories handed down through the ages are actually based in facts long forgotten. We really should explore them more deeply for their foundations.

This is an allegory of sorts that examines the 'what if' aspect of everything having some foundation in truth and reality and the possibility of it all being related. What if it is all more than we give it credit? My studies of the Bible and science have proven to me that they both are correct and coincide completely and unquestionably. My earnest belief is that those that argue against this point are simply afraid of the actual facts and the implications of such a universe. What if the Norse gods were somehow real in some respect we have yet to discover? What if the Pyramids were landing pads for alien ships or sources of electrical generation as some are now suggesting? What if it is all interrelated? Who are we to be so arrogant and narcissistic to believe that there are not multiple lines of thought that actually converge to create the reality in which we live, but none of us really understand? Why can't we question why?

This fiction/fantasy revolves around many of the gods of Greece and Egypt with a smattering of references to Biblical history and fact. Why not? Theologians will likely claim I've bastardized the gospels but you know what? Like Ricky Gervais, "I don't care." I think there is room to consider that the apocrypha should be reincorporated into the biblical text. Lillith of the apocrypha might just shed light on certain aspects of Eden, Earth, Heaven and Hell. I think that there is room to consider that the gods of Olympus and the gods of the pyramids of Egypt might actually have existed in some form at some time and that we as a race of pompous fools are unable to cope with the reality of the supernatural that is documented and laid before us. With Quarks flashing in and out of existence, is it so unlikely?

In this novel, Zeus, Danaë, Persæus and Achilles have a close-knit relationship with many actors bringing problems, solutions and comedic relief into their intertwining lives. Persæus tames the demons in his soul that Zeus gives him as a possible blessing depending on how he addresses them and treats them. They become his friends and mentors and at times, they give Zeus reason to shake his head at having given them life in his son, three persons in one. From the realization of his own existence to the complex relationships of everyday life, it is a journey of discovery and friendship that has no competition in the literary world and is unlike anything you have ever read before. It is fun, so romantic at a point toward the end, as to bring one to tears, adventurous and quite heroic in places and exceedingly thought provoking.

You'll never read anything like it as it moves you from fighting for survival to loving everyone around you and appreciating the complex relationships some of us have in loving those around us. The gods we put above us in our everyday lives and the factual information you may have never before considered. I challenge you to enjoy reading it as much as I have enjoyed writing it.

Brent J. Cole

Table of Contents

Once Upon a Midnight Deity

CHAPTER ONE: IN THE BEGINNING

The comfort and warmth of his home was something he'd always cherished and the room to move around seemed inexplicably large since the very beginning. It seemed to take forever to travel from one side to the other when he first became aware and that seemed so very long ago; almost an interminable amount of time and it had passed slowly but inexorably as he ate, slept and swam around. He'd first become aware of himself as he lost his tail and discovered his thumb.

The tail had been useful to move around but he only had the most distant memory of it as he developed other appendages and started feeling the urge to move about and stretch out. But as he did so it seemed his home, soft and warm, was becoming smaller or maybe he was growing larger, the concept was utterly foreign to him and he didn't really mind just as long as he was fed and comfortable. At times the vibrations were high and melodical and at other times, low, slow and rumbling and although they seemed comforting most of the time there was a sense of urgency at others that he did not understand. And always a babump, babump, babump, babump, babump.

As the time passed, he noticed there was activity around him over which he had no control and he could feel the accelerations and sudden stops of movement that he'd not noticed before. And there was a cycle of activity and rest that were very consistent and seemed perfectly timed to the miniscule amount of light he'd been noticing. As time passed, he became more aware that his home had become too small and his movement was restricted in a manner he'd never noticed before and it was almost uncomfortable. He sucked his thumb more and more as it seemed to be a comfort and every now and then he would try to push back the walls in an effort to stretch in the manner that he once did. It was to no avail. He began to feel restricted and wanted so very much to get away from the constraints of movement that he'd never before realized.

Then his life changed and the home that had been so large, wonderful, warm and comforting was squeezing him in a way that was almost malicious and he didn't understand as his head felt compressed and distorted and nearly painful. There were sounds around him that he didn't recognize and the warmth was not as embracing and he felt a poke at the top of his being that was sharp and kept him uncomfortable. At times the compression was so distinct and grand that he felt like he was drifting away from consciousness and then it would ease and allow him to regain an awareness of the sounds around him. So many sounds but always the two, the one sweet and melodious and the other low and rumbling, but not frightening.

Then finally he felt a few moments of squeezing that made his world go black, he felt like his life was ending and didn't know what was happening. Was this all there was to his existence? Was it over? He no longer remembered his tail but his thumbs had become so very important to his comfort and were always in his thoughts yet, now, he could not find them to put one or both in his mouth. They were constrained below somewhere and he could not raise them to suck on and his world ebbed in and out like it was under someone else's control and it was ending and starting and ending and starting. And the light! The pain of the light in his face that stabbed into the most private area of his thoughts and the ache in his chest were beyond comprehension!

"It's a boy, Mrs. Rollins!" was the calm but happy voice of the maternity nurse. "But you knew that already, didn't you?

WHAT? Didn't you have any idea at all? NO! Why not? A surprise? Well, are you surprised?"

"Let me see my baby," said the melodious voice he had come to recognize as being there always.

"Here you go sweety, he seems to be pecking," was the response from the low rumbling sound he knew so well.

He felt something in his mouth, not his thumb but something with a distinct stimulation that he'd never had before and he knew somehow this was right and he didn't need his thumbs right now. Strange word, "thumbs." And how did he know that?

"Do you know what you'll name him?"

"We don't have a name picked out yet," said Mrs. Rollins. "We were thinking maybe Persæus"

"What an intriguing name. Does it have special meaning?"

"It was his grandfather's name in Latin"

"Would that be your father or Mr. Rollins' father?"

"You ask too many questions," said Mr. Rollins and with that he dispatched all those in the delivery room with one swipe of his clawed hand. There could be no witnesses to the birth of such a bastard. "Shall we go home?" he asked.

The delivery had been successful and Danaë was already healing, she agreed, "Of course Zeus."

With that the three disappeared in a mist of wind that swirled up and out through the ceiling.

The child of such a union would be strong indeed and he grew with a rapidity that stunned even his parents. Zeus was not one to stick around as he had so many offspring by so many strange loves. But this child intrigued him with his extreme prowess in all that he attempted. All Zeus' children clamored for his favor. Such was the fate of a god among gods and the original deadbeat dad by modern definition. But not so Persæus, he seemed to be more adept at being alone and in fact, seemed to take a particular pleasure in being so. He was especially skilled at hunting and was the most stealthy of any child that Zeus had ever observed. It seemed that way because his long legs were like iron and he could stop cold and wait for an hour squatted and ready to bound after his prey.

Persæus loved to hunt in the hills stalking deer and even bear. He could track and he could run like an antelope jumping even small valleys and downed trees. He was especially adept at running the grape fields and jumping the rows of grapes as though they were hurtles and it was his second nature. Zeus sometimes watched him from above and not being as cold hearted as he was reputed, he was quite proud of this bastard son of his. The boy had potential to be more of a god than a man and he was interested to see how he would turn out. Only Zeus knew the wonderful possibilities of his conception and existence, the spirits in his soul that would serve to guide him in a life of adventure and wonderment.

He was a predatory child in every respect right down to his long feet and iron grip. No one and nothing dared challenge Persæus as just looking at his formidable stature was enough to drive off any sane person, demigod, child or adult. Even at his young age of sixteen he could drink with the best of the men and he was known to be quite a cantankerous fighter even when he could barely stand from the alcohol. Those were the times that made Zeus chuckle as he watched him down men twice his age that had much more experienced while reeling drunk on one foot at times. It was better than watching a jester.

That didn't mean he was not well liked; he had an affinity for befriending the most beautiful of the young girls of the island where he and his mother lived and his valor was beyond reproach. There was just something about him that had everyone just a bit frightened of him, especially if someone unwittingly angered him. He stood a head taller than most and there was a red glow that would rise up behind his eyes and his voice would drop an octave with a gravely roughness that belied the violence hiding just under the surface. The people of the island of Seriphos gathered before king Polydectes and in fear asked that Persæus be banned from their home, at least for a time until he matured. King Polydectes succumbed to their fervent supplication albeit with trepidation of some retribution even apologizing to Persaeus and Danaë. Zeus stood by and watched from the shadows to observe this inhuman bonding of god and man, the Nephilim of scripture of which some men wrote.

Persæus and Danaë left the island of Seriphos for a time vowing to return someday to reunite with friends and family but with king Polydectes' permission of course. Greece had become a buzzing metropolis and the simple clothing of their previous island home stood out and made the two of them a center of attention. It seemed the gold coin of Seriphos was coveted but the people wanted to trade in paper notes that held no value in the eyes of any sane person. They found a bank with which they were familiar even in their own home and found those in charge were quite happy to help them convert their gold to the necessary paper and a flexible card they called plastic. They were assured it would be well accepted as payment anywhere in the world.

It had been many decades since Persæus had been born but his age was only sixteen as he understood it. He had to have Danaë's permission to do anything in this strange place. A place that was different even to Danaë from the day she had given birth. It was almost as though time passed differently here from the island of Seriphos. The hospital in which she had given birth to her son was no longer where it had been and when she asked a passerby, she had been told it was destroyed in a world war some time ago. They were both confused in this world and stayed close together in order to avoid any possible trouble. It was unlikely that anyone would bother Persæus with his stunning good looks and huge presence standing at nearly seven feet tall.

But his gorgeous mother attracted a great deal of attention from passing men who were of low origin and pursued her with cat calls and strange requests befitting a whore. It was all Persæus could do to contain himself and not rip off their heads as he knew he was quite capable. At one point, Danaë held him back by his arm as he faltered and went to pursue a group of men that were foolish enough to start following them with obscene comments. When she did so, she felt his arm become engorged and swollen as though he was morphing into something larger and more vile. When he turned to her upon stopping, she saw the red in his eyes of which the populous of Seriphos had so often gossiped from fear. Persæus loved his mother so much he never let her see that side of himself but this land of men that had no decency had him on an edge so fine he was without his normal control.

They found a tenement for a pittance the owner called a suite. Persæus did not see it as being anything more than a hovel but Danaë assured him it was fully adequate and they should be happy it was available to them without any references. He deferred to his mother's wisdom in this strange world of which he was unfamiliar with its bustling covered carts that carried only one passenger. The roaring that emanated from the rear of those carts that seemed so inefficient and noisy was especially bothersome in the night time while trying to sleep. It was a dirty place yet it was full of surprises and strange wonderments that caused him to ask many questions of his mother and of strangers passing by. He was put off by the unfriendliness of those strangers but so many seemed to be in an extreme hurry and he could not understand why. Danaë explained it was the need for them to earn a living that made them as they were. Persæus had never had that issue as his father made sure he had all that he needed in his previous life. Danaë mentioned he would likely have to find a trade at some point as their gold, though quite abundant, would not last forever. He did not find that to be probable, but he assured her he would start looking for something that he wished to do.

He felt he could do anything to which he set his mind but if push came to shove, he likely could find gainful employment at the docks doing almost anything. With his height and strength, he was capable of most any manual labor. The question in his mind that he did not express to his mother was whether or not they would pay him his value and if it would be in gold or the worthless paper they seemed to value here. The first week he accompanied his mother about town as she found sheets, towels plates, furniture and cooking needs with which to fill their suite. Persæus suggested his mother find a maid to help with these things but she assured him that she did not need that kind of help. Back on Seriphos they were of the royal family and this style of life was very foreign to him. His mother assured him it would be a good and a growing experience for him to understand how most of the world outside of their island kingdom lived. A manner of which he had never become aware in his childhood.

As the men around the neighborhood began to become accustomed to seeing the two of them together, they became less obnoxious and even started greeting them in a manner proper to people of royal lineage. Persæus started learning the names of some of the older gents that showed respect for his mother and would even converse on occasion, especially if they seemed to know of gainful employment. He learned of a business in the neighborhood that busied itself with what the men called fabrication and welding that they felt he might fit right in. They asked if he had any welding experience and he admitted that he had none. The older gent that suggested the shop told Persæus he would check with his friend that owned the place to see if he might have something Persæus could do for him. Persæus showed the proper gratitude and respect for the man as his mother had taught him and the next day Gustov told him to go see his friend at the fabrication and welding shop near the waterfront. He said it was called The Works. Gustov said to ask for Achilles. It was odd that this man he was to seek had the same name as his deceased cousin.

Persæus didn't wait until the next day as one might expect but went immediately after what might be the midday meal. Hoping to catch Achilles in a good state after eating. He knew they did not yet need the money but he wanted to get to know these people in this land. To have human interaction and learn more of their mundane existence where they could not hunt the area due to so much population. Hunting was what he was beginning to miss more than anything and he hoped that someone at The Works would have a line on a place to do so.

When he arrived, he was somewhat impressed with the men he saw working as they seemed to be strong and well-toned for this city that seemed so intent upon relaxation and drinking. Not that he minded drinking but he tended to get into trouble as there were few that could tolerate his arrogant mouth when the alcohol took hold. It was something on which he had to watch himself. So, as much as he enjoyed it, like so many, he stayed away from the taverns. He had already trounced many good men because of his size and his errant speech when he'd had too much to drink; at least a part of the reason he'd been asked to leave Seriphos. He laughed to himself but he knew he could not afford to make enemies. He asked for Achilles of the first man he saw that was not carrying a load. He was directed to a room at the back of the building that had a closed door and an air conditioner.

He knocked on the door and a man that looked vaguely familiar waved him in.

"Gustov called and told me you were on your way over. Did he have the story straight? Are you Persæus from Seriphos?"

"Yes, I am are you my cousin, Achilles?"

"Yes, I am! What are the chances that we should meet like this? Pretty high if you know the tale."

"I don't get it. Why are you here among the mortals? Everyone thinks you're dead!"

"Close the door. Zeus took pity on me for some unknown reason, he didn't allow me to die from a superficial wound; why would an arrow in my heel kill me? Ask yourself, does that sound like a mortal wound?"

"It was a false flag narrative that was used to satiate Paris and end the conflict; it also exposed Apollo as an enemy of the gods for guiding the arrow. But how does one do away with the great purifier? That guy has such a goodie two shoes reputation, and the reality is that he just doesn't have what it takes to make the ladies happy and that makes him an over achiever trying to compensate. So, Zues told me to come here for eternity and honestly, once I got used to it, it's not so bad."

"Seriously, that's your story?"

"And I'm sticking to it!"

"I would never have expected this. Do you think this is all just coincidence?"

"My blood, there is no such thing as coincidence. It is all plans and schemes and it was never left up to chance. You are here because I heard you had come to town. You were sent to this town because I'm here. The powers that be, knew this and manipulated this. And you are big news. Who else is seven feet tall with a goddess of a mortal for a mother?"

"Well, Zeus thought so, at least. Her beauty is why I exist today. Surprisingly he's still hanging around from time to time."

"Oh, he will. He likes to meddle in not just human affairs but in those of all his subjects. And sometimes he does a pretty good job of things. Crazy old fart."

At just that moment, a bolt of lightning thundered across the sky and both men laughed as they knew Zeus had a sense of humor; but eyeing each other, they didn't push their luck either. Being all powerful did not escape his repertoire of tricks being also eternal; but they did not wish to earn his ire as he was of good humor most of the time and they liked to keep it that way.

"All right, dad, we know you're listening always."

Both men smiled and chuckled as in their heads they heard the

voice of Zeus as he said, "Just keep that in mind, boys."
They both knew Zeus was usually very benevolent unlike the poets and minstrels made him out to be. But they always made him out to have human flaws when in fact he was a god and most of the time he acted quite god like in all manners one might expect. And then there was the hospital of Persæus' birth... That hadn't been very benevolent of him but there couldn't be any witnesses and Zeus knew that at least most of those humans would die shortly in an errant German buzz bomb explosion. After all, death is death whether by god or by man. It still made one wonder about Zeus' temper.

And so, the man-boy Persæus and his cousin reunited in the land of men and Persæus began working at The Works learning a trade of men and becoming friends with many there at his place of employment. He was quite disappointed they did not pay his wages in gold. Everyone wanted gold but no one was giving it as payment in this strange land. They gave him a piece of paper that they told him had value if he went to his bank and gave it to them. He learned it was a promissory note that would allow him to buy gold at an inflated price which he would have to wait and see if it became valued accordingly. It was indeed a strange land and although he didn't like their system of monetary compensation, it had its own strange harmony with his soul and he was intrigued. He was thankful to King Polydectes for banishing him to learn of this land and its customs and to Zeus for placing the thought in the heads of the people of the island of Seriphos. It was all about attitude and he was learning why his mother was so patient over the decisions made for her and this life which she accepted as normal after living a life of royalty.

So many rebelled against the gods and their whims when it was so much easier to learn from them and their ways. Persæus was not always happy with what they provided but he had his loving mother and his cousin to guide him and his father to provide wisdom and new adventures as he saw fit. In reality, he was living the good life he had not expected outside of the royal family on Seriphos and he admitted to himself, his mother and his cousin, Achilles, and by proxy, his father, that he was beginning to understand this laborious life of the human condition more than he had expected. He was coming to understand what Achilles had meant when he said it wasn't so bad once one became used to it. He reveled in the physicality of the job and he enjoyed the companionship of these trifling coworkers whom, in a manner, he was coming to respect.

So many had families, and some quite large, very much like his father and they all loved their offspring and did whatever they could to provide for the ones that appreciated them. It was not LIKE being among the gods, these people, in many respects, were the gods here on earth. They just weren't omniscient, omnipresent, eternal and all powerful; okay, not quite gods, but they did have a presence that was immutable. He was understanding why his father watched over them as he did. Most had long forgotten about him but he had not and would not forget about them and never would or even could; it was not in him to forget about them even when disappointed.

The work continued at The Works and Persæus was relatively happy in comparison to his previous life. He especially enjoyed the attention he received from the girls in the area, many calling him tree top lover, not that he ever did, regardless that they were quite tempting at times. He spoke many times with Achilles about hunting and when the day came that they closed the shop for holiday, Achilles agreed and Persæus could hardly contain himself. There was a place outside the city in the hills of which Achilles was aware and he promised Persæus that they would go and enjoy a few days of time together. Several of the men of the shop were also going so it would be a time not only of hunting but of revelry and bonding among the men.

CHAPTER TWO:
THE HUNT

Achilles assured Persæus there would be game in the area they were going to visit and was sure to help him find the necessary tools to bring down the animals he intended to hunt. They loaded up one of the company flatbeds that had removable side rails which they installed and a group of them from work set off on a Friday evening to a place they called the valley. As they were on the shore themselves that meant traveling into the hill country in order to have a valley in which to hunt. But Persæus wasn't to be disappointed as the lush green undergrowth showed great promise of probable game in that some of the greenery had been consumed and the game trails were obvious to even the untrained eye.

They had departed before dawn from The Works in order to reach their destination and scope out a place that was hospitable to humans and close enough to the wilderness to afford ample exposure to game animals. Achilles mentioned there would probably be many humans partaking of the same adventures of this weekend and to be watchful not to bag one of them; although that might be funny to hang on the wall at work.
"Watch that humor boys," came Zeus' familiar voice to them both. He did not make his presence known often but it was always with wisdom and occasionally with humor. They smiled and gently slugged each other in the shoulder knowing they would not make that mistake.

Achilles knew of a small clearing on a stream where the animals tended to lose their fear of humans and would go to drink in the mornings and evenings. He recommended to the group to set up camp on a ledge about thirty feet above and on East side to take advantage of the morning sun. That, of course, would not help in the evenings but they could see places of cover across the way where thy might assume positions for the evening hunt. This might work for the first night or even two, but the animals would become wary if their numbers were to be diminished greatly and there would be the smell of blood and death at the watering hole. They hoped to bag their limit quickly and quietly such that the animals would not be aware of their success. It would be a premium position if they could set up on the Northern side but the stream that fed the area washed down the side of a fairly vertical precipice that didn't appear to afford access for hunters to hide. The southern exposure was just that, exposed so that was not an option either. They would just make do with what they had as that wasn't so bad, regardless.

They set up camp about thirty meters away on the Eastern side and as evening approached Persæus couldn't help but feel drawn to the far side of the clearing, He quietly left the main party and set himself in the brush near the pond on the West side where he hunkered down to await the animals. His blood was running hot for the hunt and he could not help but leave the rest at camp to hunt on his own. He waited quietly hunkered down hearing the water and the birds of the area smelling the air distinctly fresh from the scent of the city. Although he could feel his heart in his chest he was breathing slowly and steadily as a fawn and a doe came to the clearing. These were not the Dama-Dama of Rhodes but Red Fallow deer that were once held sacred by the goddess Artemis and four had been harnessed to her chariot. Persæus could hear the buck as it waited in the bushes to see if it was safe, stomping from time to time and snorting with impatience.

Finally, the cowardly buck ventured out and stood beside the doe and fawn as they drank, his head upright sniffing the air.

He obviously smelled the hunters' camp, strange but somehow familiar and knew things were more dangerous than usual. As the two had their fill of the fresh water the doe stood guard and the buck took his turn to drink mightily and that was when Persæus struck. With his dagger between his teeth, he sprang from his hide, arms outstretched directly for the buck. This was a large animal possibly as much as 200 kilos (450 lbs.) dwarfing Persæus but quick none the less. It was good that Persæus was only a couple of meters away, even so the large animal was up and spun on him before he could reach it and in surprise and fear, raised up on its hind legs rather than lowering its head for a fight. When Persæus hit the animal in the chest at a full speed lunge, it was like hitting a brick wall. He knocked the wind out of himself but managed to move the animal over backward. And grabbing the dagger from his teeth he plunged it deep between the animal's ribs and moved the tip in four directions hoping to take an artery and make short work of it.

His aim was amiss by only a fraction and as he tried to find an artery the big buck was biting at his head and kicking him with his hooves violently and mercilessly. It rolled out from under him but in doing so ended his own life as the dagger twisted and sliced into some major supply of blood and jumping, it took but two faltering steps and fell dead. The doe and fawn were long gone but Persæus had the first kill and he swelled with pride that he had not had to use an arrow but tackled the king of the forest with only his dagger. His attack might not normally elicit anything more than a grunt from a buck but this one had screamed as they sometimes do when startled.

The camp, had come running toward the sound that was loud and shrill. Across the pond were the murmurs of the other hunters as they surveyed the scene with shock and awe. Persæus beckoned them to come over and help him take the beast back closer to camp to bleed and gut it such that it would not spoil the area with the scent of death making it unlikely to see more game at this spot. He wished he could quarter the animal right here to make transporting it easier but that could wait the few minutes necessary to clear the area. They trussed it over a pair of strong branches crossed in an X such that four men including Persæus were able to carry it to a place they felt would be suitable to cut it up. It had already bled into the chest cavity but the neck was sliced under the jaw anyway to ensure a complete drain of fluid. Persæus made short work of the quartering and gutting which he covered over with dirt and leaves to reduce the stench which might develop before they broke camp. They hung the quarters high in the trees to keep the other animals from spoiling the meat.

The heart, stomach and liver were kept for cooking over the fire that evening and they all had some of the kill before retiring. It was a good hunt already and now everyone was on fire for their own kill. By the time he was falling asleep, the bite wounds in his scalp were already coagulated and healing and he knew he would soon be as right as rain; the dried blood already falling from his face. He would wash himself below the pond after the morning hunt and well before dusk such that he wouldn't disturb any animals and the scent would float away with the moving water. He drifted off to a comfortable and fulfilled slumber before the rest of the camp and did not get to hear how some were angered that he'd bagged the first kill. He probably would not have cared anyway.

The dawn came and several men were already out sculking around in the brush and a few had tried to find a spot above the pond with a vantage point. Persæus decided to stay in camp this morning as his thirst for the first kill had been satiated and he might be needed to help pack out someone else's kill. He cut a slice from a hind quarter very thin and fried it like bacon with some lard they'd brought with them. It made for a very tasty breakfast and some hard biscuits his mother had sent with him dipped in the drippings, followed by strawberries; they were the icing on the cake. The fare while hunting was different in many ways from most days but that only meant it tasted that much better. Persæus decided to have lunch ready for the others from the supplies they'd brought along but with the bonus of some of the meat from his kill. He decided it would be good to boil the meat with vegetables for a stew with barley. Somehow that just felt and sounded so right for the first hunt in this new world; he was not wrong and the men were plenty grateful. They forgot completely at how they were jealous of him getting the first animal.

After lunch Persæus walked to the outflow of the pond and then a bit further and Achilles went with him. He wanted to wash the dried blood from his hair and whatever might remain on his face; he could feel it pull at his skin. Achilles spoke with him about going off alone to make the first kill and how it may not have been the best way to make friends.

"You didn't really do anything wrong, but I think it made you stand out more than you should, especially with you being almost seven feet tall already. And being the cousin of the owner adds a bit of jealousy to the mix anyway."

"I suppose you're right; I was simply compelled to be in the woods alone, it's something I've always done and I was driven to make a kill."

"Are you feeling better now?"

"Much, it was a relief to tackle that big buck with my bare hands."

"Is that something you are also accustomed to doing? Do you do that with bears also?"

"Well, not so much bears, not since the first time I tried it. That gets pretty rough and my fast healing would be difficult to explain away in this world."

"I'm wondering, Persæus, if there is something else going on that no one realizes. Normally I come to your shoulder and last night after your kill you were most definitely a couple of inches taller. I wrote it off to the exhilaration of the kill, standing tall, but today you're back to the height I expect. You grow with your level of violence."

"Mother mentioned the other day that my arm swelled when I was antagonized by some men that were rude to her. She swore I got bigger as well."

Persæus washed his face and hair in the stream as they spoke.

"You know," said Achilles, "those Christians wrote of a creature they called a Nephilim that is a cross breed between their so-called angels and human women. They are large and violent and you, my cousin, kind of fit into that category. Has your father ever spoken to you about these things?"

"Not at all, but he does seem to keep closer tabs on me than his other myriads of offspring. I've often wondered at that as we are not particularly close, but I feel his presence quite often. Dad, are you listening?"

"He's listening, I feel him also. I think he wants you to figure this out without his help."

There was thunder in the distance that made them both consider that possibility to be the fact of the matter.

"Maybe that is why we have been thrown together as we have. I believe you are intended to be my mentor."

"Well, I am happy to guide you with what little wisdom I have but remember, I was responsible for the ten-year Trojan war and I claimed the life of Hector. It was not a pretty sight and everyone was plenty angry with me for dragging Hector's body around behind my chariot. One of those things in my life I wish I could undo but, it is what it is and I live with it."

"Maybe that is why you are perfect to help me grow while I'm here; you know victory, battle, regret and so many things that maybe you can help me understand and avoid so much, if that should be the case."

"I think you give me too much credit, but I'm here for you if that is what you think you want. You were always one of my favorite cousins anyway. I was always grateful to Zeus for letting me sneak back and visit with you and some of my other relatives. I had to keep it on the down low and it was not as often as I would have liked; but it was appreciated."

"You're welcome," came the voice of Zeus in their heads.

They had reached the encampment at this point and it was time to put aside the conversations of centuries past so the other men would have no reason to suspect the nature of their origins. It was often difficult enough to explain conversations accidentally overheard without adding fuel to the fire. One of the men had shot a spike buck clean through the heart and they already had it dressed before Persæus and Achilles got back to camp. There was enough of the stew left for the man known as Joseph so he was well filled in addition to getting his kill. The spike was hung in the branches next to the quarters of Persæus kill. So far it was a very successful hunt and it promised to be better yet as Persæus and Achilles prayed to Zeus for a blessing on the rest of the men for their success also.

Persæus thought long that afternoon about what Achilles had said about the Nephilim and his apparent growth when angered or violent. It seemed to have logic and he couldn't overlook that his mother had also noticed it. He had felt himself changing within as he had grown older; from about the time he was thirteen he felt strange emotions and almost like vibrations or rumblings within, especially during the hunt that he loved so much. He knew he was very different from other demi-gods but he could not fathom the divergence and Zeus had not been inclined to help him understand. His hope was that Achilles could help him, being so much older and more experienced and he may have just opened his eyes to something he knew but had not yet recognized. Was he changing in a manner that might not be wholesome? It was a bit frightening in that he felt he might be dangerous to those around him including his mother and cousin. The evening hunt was upon them shortly and he decided to walk around and see if he could flank some game toward the pond. He asked Joseph to walk with him, he was not accustomed to having company on the hunt but he liked this man.

Both men had spotted their kills on the far side of the pond so they determined there might be a heavily used game trail on that side. They climbed around the upstream side of the water and headed in an oversize arch both beyond and upstream of the areas where they'd both made their kills. They spoke quietly as they walked knowing that although voices carried, it was amazing how quickly they would fall quiet in the dense undergrowth and the leaf covered floor of the forest. They had both stumbled upon prey in the past that had only stopped to observe their passage before attending to what they'd been previously doing. So, they spoke softly as they proceeded stepping gently to reduce the disturbance of their presence. Joseph had been working for Achilles for almost a decade and respected him in a surprising manner.

"He has always treated me fairly and paid me on time. I have no complaints against the man; regardless of the fact that you two are cousins, I would speak my mind openly if there was anything that needed to be said. Of course, I'd speak to him first and foremost. I don't believe I should do otherwise as that would be back stabbing."

"I can appreciate that in a person, I feel the same way. I have known Achilles my entire life even though we did not always see much of each other, especially the past few years as it was rumored he'd been killed in a great fight. We had little more information than that and I had never had the opportunity to look for him. It was providence that brought us together in this town."

"In a good year he has even given us a bonus; that is almost unheard of in our town and everyone appreciates that, maybe more than we have expressed."

"He has his faults but his heart is good and he will stand by a good man without question. I'm glad you are happy with him as an employer, I know he appreciates all of his men or you would not still be around."

"He is my friend, also, we have had many good times together.

My wife wants to set him up with her cousin but he does not seem interested in women, or men for that matter; thank the gods."

"My mother has told me he has had love interests in the past but it will take a very special person to sway him from his celibacy. Well, I'm assuming he has been celibate but there are many things about him I don't know firsthand."

At that point they had come to a pair of ridges with a shallow valley in between that paralleled the stream feeding their pond. They decided that Joseph would walk the far ridge while Achilles walked the shallow valley and try to drive any game across toward where the other men were hunting. As they walked slowly in the direction of the hunting party, Joseph had mulled over the things he and Persæus had discussed about Achilles. It seemed there was great love between the men albeit not having seen much of each other over the years. He wondered if familiarity would breed contempt or if their family bond was stronger than that. It seemed that they might be closer than many families and he had high hopes for them both as he felt a comradery with them both and he felt comfortable with them as friends.

At that point there was a great trashing from behind and below where they were walking toward the hunting party. It was obvious that something had spooked a herd and it was headed their way if they were savvy enough to get behind it. Both men paused and listened as it came closer and at the same moment, they both saw where a major game trail passed across the area heading toward the pond. Persæus was climbing the slope to meet with Joseph and fall in behind the herd. It wasn't long before the animals had covered the distance and were now visible to the two men. They stood in silent patience waiting for the animals to pass hoping they would not be noticed. As they passed, Persæus was in hot pursuit with Joseph not far behind, Persæus running with his long legs easily keeping pace. They were running not so much to scare the animals as they were already traveling at a full gallop, but rather just to be there in case they needed to redirect the herd toward the hunting party.

It was a merry chase but soon they neared the watering pond and Persæus cautioned Joseph to slow down and let the herd go ahead. Joseph was breathing hard at this point anyway, Persæus not so much for his long legs were an asset. Persæus mentioned he didn't know the skill of the men with their bows well enough to get much closer when their arrows were loosed upon the herd. Joseph laughed softly as his thoughts had moved in the same direction. But soon they could see animals falling and a few shouts from the men to startle the deer into stopping and looking for the source of the noise. It was a thing of beauty as they heard a shout, the herd would slow and even stop and animals would fall. Then lurching into action again as a unified front the deer would start moving again and another man would shout from another direction, the animals again were stopping; more would fall. Finally, the herd was allowed to move on or maybe they just quit paying attention to the shouts but they were gone as quickly as they had arrived. Persæus and Joseph moved in to help the men bleed and gut their trophies as there was no worry about spoiling the area now that all had bagged their animals. It was a good day for the hunters but the herd; not so much.

Several of the animals were large enough to need quartering and it took a few trips back and forth to get all the carcasses back to camp and hung in the trees. They would all have plenty to feed their families for the next couple of months and there was a celebration to be had in the camp that evening. Persæus gave up a quarter of his prize to Joseph as he had shot the spike and had young children; it only seemed right. It helped to make solid the bond they were developing and it just felt good to do something nice for another human being. The men got busy bringing down quarters of the meet, slicing and salting a good deal of it to preserve it. They made racks on which to hang the salted meat close to the fire pit such that it would help to dry the meat and also to keep an eye on it as the forest animals might be tempted. Another pot of stew was started and the wine and liquor flowed early that day. Although they'd done little, Persæus and Joseph were lauded for guiding the stampeding herd into the hunting party and then for their help in dressing the animals.

Persæus ate well that afternoon and thanked Zeus for blessing their hunt. Zeus did not always listen when Persæus asked for a favor but he came through in aces this time. He thought further of what he and Achilles had discussed of the Nephilim and surmised that possibly Zeus might not be a god in and of himself. Rather he might be an angel that he had procreated with so many human women. Persæus didn't even know how many half brothers and sisters he actually had. He tried to think back and account for all that he had heard of and that his mother had related to him but it made his head hurt. Mixing wine and liquor was not helping in that respect either. He would have to slow down if he didn't want to wind up fighting with someone that might otherwise be a best friend.

One of the men had brought a mandolin and began playing his best tunes for the others. Another had brought a drum of sorts and still a third had a flute. It was surprisingly well coordinated and every one enjoyed the make shift band and even danced to a few of the tunes. Persæus was certain the alcohol helped with the dancing and made it appear almost good. He had not suspected the drum as the man had brought food and clothing in it. It appeared he had hollowed out a very small log with fire and scraping and he changed the sound of it by tapping either on one end or the side. What was unique was the use of dog or possibly wolf femurs for drum sticks.

Persæus even danced to a few of the tunes but being such a giant among the others he felt a bit out of place. Still the alcohol made him jolly and he kept himself in check so as not to offend or make himself a pariah. It wasn't long until he was ready to call it a night and he went to bed. The others were up making noise but he fell out without a second thought. He dreamed of the hunt and naked women; after all he was now seventeen.

CHAPTER THREE:
A MOTHER'S
EXPLANATION

The sun was well up as the men began to move around the camp. Many were moving quite slowly as the night's debauchery had been a bit much for them. Persæus did not feel badly although he didn't want to roll out quite yet, but the movement in the camp was too much for him to continue sleeping. Someone had already stoked the fire and a giant pot of coffee was on the boil. The smell was enough to make him crave it and he understood why so many succumbed to its addiction. A bitter drink but so tasty with honey it soothed even the worst of mornings and made them palatable. Someone had brought loaves of bread with butter and set them above the fire to warm and melt the scent making him salivate and crave sustenance. Pieces were now cut and laying there for everyone to partake and enjoy. The same honey for the coffee went well on the homemade loaves and soon everyone was satiated and conversing about the previous day's hunt and the night of celebration. They would soon pack up camp as they all had plenty of meat and needed to get it home, some to freeze and the rest to finish salt curing.

Before long, the men packed up their bounty and their belongings and loaded up the truck. The journey home was not a long one but many wanted to have their meat attended and their gear stowed before lunch so they could enjoy the afternoon with their families. They would all return to work the next morning and regardless of being out with the boss, they were all expected to be well rested and show up at work on time. Some of the men knew they would need to address a honey do list once they returned home although their wives might go easy on them considering the gifts they brought. It gave new meaning to the trojan saying, "Beware of Greeks bearing gifts." Many of the younger men might be called upon by their wives to perform other necessary duties.

The morning was brisk and Persæus covered himself with a shawl as he seldom needed a coat but the wind that blew around to the back of the truck made him rethink his need. He would survive the ride home and he could hardly wait to tell his mother of his talk with Achilles. He wondered what her response might be to the possibility of him being a Nephilim or something there about. On the day they headed out for the hunt they had simply met up at The Works and loaded into the truck but because of the haul of meat the driver took them each to their individual homes. As he got off the truck Achilles hopped out of the front and shook his hand and mentioned he should speak to his mother about that which they had spoken. He then hugged his giant cousin and jumped into the back to talk with his crew; a crew of friends that he valued greatly.

Persæus felt he had made good inroads with the crew, especially Joseph; and he felt this was like a new understanding for both the crew and for himself. He was looking forward to his time in the near future hoping to foster the feeling of friendship and respect he'd felt over the holiday. He was hard pressed to ask his petit mother for help with the meat so he moved everything to the door and then placed it inside the door on the floor. He walked in and found his mother knitting; something he had never seen her do as the daughter of a king and he never knew she was skilled in that manner. Expressing his surprise to her she smiled and said, "There are so many things you don't know about me. Someday I may surprise you again. Let me help you with your things. The salted meat can go on the back porch, I have racks set up already anticipating your success. And I can smell the pelts and blood. You can use the table out there to cut up what you haven't salted and we'll wash it down after. Will you be hungry soon?"

"Yes, mother. We had bread and coffee for breakfast but I was hoping you wouldn't mind cooking some loukaniko sausage and eggs?"

"Of course! If you haven't had your fill of venison already you can leave some steaks in the refrigerator to use for dinner tonight as well."

"Of course, mother, I'll even cook for you at dinner."

"I would expect nothing less of the mighty hunter."

They smiled at their banter and Persæus was filled with love for the beautiful soul in this woman that had given him life.

Persæus carried what was left of the quarters out to the back porch and laid them on the table. He unwrapped the salted meat and salted it again before laying it over the racks. He then began the process of cutting the rest into roasts, fillets and steaks to wrap for the freezer. He was looking forward to barbequing the ribs sometime soon. Being a very lean rack of ribs his uncles, back on Seriphos, had taught him to soak them in a light brine with turbinado sugar and use a mixture of olive oil and butter to cook them so they wouldn't dry so badly that they might become tough. He salivated just thinking of the tender flavor of such a feast.

Danaë called Persæus to his brunch and as he approached, he noticed a bit of buttered bread to go with his sausage and eggs. He'd be getting fat if he ate like this all the time but they both knew he had worked hard to make the trip a success.

"Mother, Achilles and I were talking and he brought up something interesting about which I wanted to speak to you."

"Hmmm, I can just imagine coming from Achilles," she said with a knowing smile.

"Oh, it's nothing terrible but he also noticed that I seem to get larger with violence, in this case, the hunt. Just as you noticed when those men angered me."

"Yes, it is of concern to me also. I hope you haven't found yourself becoming uncontrolled?"

"No more than usual, mother," he said teasingly.

"Go on…"

"Well, he suggested there may be a connection with the Nephilim of the Christians and suggested I might be of a nature to change under certain duress. Are you aware of the Nephilim?"

"Yes, and they did exist and some still do exist. I don't know that you are of the same nature but there is a distinct possibility that you have certain predispositions of your nature due to your father. I suspect you will be realizing them as you come of age and you need to be aware and prepared for whatever they might be."

"Is there no way of knowing?"

"I have my suspicions and you should also. You grow, you have an affinity for hunting, you can run like the wind, you have a temper that you must strive to control as you come by it almost supernaturally. There are signs that point to your need for the stimulation more of the wild than of the city. Are you beginning to understand what I'm thinking?"

"Mother, am I to become a Lycan?"

"I don't know, Zeus seems cruel at times, he has his reasons. I don't think he did this to you purposely as he did to King Lycæus. Sometimes things just happen. He might have been thinking of Lycæus when he showered me with gold, giving me such a beautiful loving son. Who knows what things happen in the mind of Zeus? Only he can tell you and only you can ask him to do that."

"Then I will do so immediately. I can't understand what he wants of me if I don't know who and what I really am."

"I think that is a wise course of action, but don't be disappointed if he doesn't answer you right away. Sometime he requires one to be patient."

"Very good, mother. I'll go finish processing the venison and then I will spend the necessary time in prayer."

"Very good. If he doesn't answer right away, let me know and I will see if he wishes to speak to me..."

"Thank you, mother."

"I will answer the boy for your sake, I do not want him to be frustrated by my machinations," said Zeus in Danaë's mind. "He deserves to know and I'll have him speak to you about it."

"Thank you, Zeus."

"Of course."

It had been years since Zeus had spoken to Danaë and it startled her a bit. His was not a voice one could easily forget but she was not sure at first if she was lucid when he spoke. But his habit of having Persæus speak to her for him was all too familiar even though it had been years since the last time he had done so. She simply waited patiently to find out what his explanation to Persæus would be and for the moment, Persæus was tending to his kill. He would be done soon enough and then he might be able to tell her at dinner. Danaë felt a bit slighted he had not spoken too her sooner, but still, she was happy that he had done so at all; he was quite busy after all and she had no right to expect him to come at her beck and call. She did hope that he would be closer to their son and maybe this was the time that might draw them together to some extent.

Persæus was just finished washing the meat and had started wrapping for the freezer when he felt Zeus' presence in his mind. "Yes, father. Have you come to speak to me?"

"Yes, Persæus, I heard you speaking to your mother. It is time I speak to you of our coming of age."

Zeus appeared before him, something he had done only a handful of times.

He appeared as any man might and truly not what one might expect from a god of Olympus but there was no doubt it was him with his customary golden crown of olive leaves. He always wore that and Persæus smiled a bit thinking it might be a matter of pride.

"Watch that thought, son. It is my right as king of Olympus and I will exercise that right regardless. You should be happy I don't turn you into a dog instead of a wolf for your insolence."

Persæus knew that Zeus was half serious so he tried to straighten up his act but he just couldn't. This was his father and although he couldn't say he loved him as one might a regular father, he did respect him and was amused at the same time.

"All right, now that's enough out of you, Persæus. I came here in good faith to explain to you about yourself. At least show a little respect for your old man."

"You know I respect you father. It's just that at times you strike me in a funny way. I do not mean to offend you by my twisted sense of humor."

"All right, I understand as I too was young once."

"You remember that far back?"

Zeus just looked at Persæus sideways, he knew it was an irresistible dig when he made the statement.

"It's a good thing I love all of my errant children… Son, about your gifts. I call them gifts as they make you special in very many ways. You are stronger than most any man and even most demi-gods. You are fast, aggressive, handsome and wise beyond your years. You have so many skills of the hunt and fighting which others can only dream. You heal quickly when wounded and you can grow to meet any challenge; and I quite literally mean grow. It's no anomaly, that is an intentional trait for your kind."

"What do you mean, my kind, father? Am I a Nephilim?"

"You are a Nephilim, a Lycanthrope and even more. You are Persæus the Ravager and Destroyer, but you are also great in wisdom and charity. You proved your charity with Joseph this recent holiday. You sought wisdom from Achilles, although I'm not sure why, I've never found him to be particularly wise. But he loves you, he is a sound and basically good man and he will be very helpful in your journey into manhood as he will be one of your closest friends."

"Father, what do you expect of me with these so called, gifts? What am I to do with these traits you call good?"

"Oh, I never called them good, they are only gifts. It is you and your spirit that must make them good. If you choose, they can be very evil. So, I admonish you to choose wisely and with a tender spirit. It will not be too long now that you will become fully enveloped in your animalistic, shape shifting self and you will have to decide to follow the inherent murderous instincts or to be the man your mother has raised you to be. You will change at will after a time of practice. But do not let the allure entice you to stay that way or you could lose yourself. You will have to make that choice in your heart and your mind around the time of your eighteenth birthday. That is when you will come fully into your gifts. As far as knowing what to do with those gifts, you will know when the time comes. I cannot tell you what will befall you, but you will know exactly what to do."

And with that, Zeus was gone from vision and Persæus could no longer feel his presence. He called out, "Thanks, Dad!" Somewhat to mock Zeus but he also meant it and was grateful as he heard the thunder roll in the distance. At least Zeus let him have some fun and banter with him. Many fathers were not of a mind to do such things and he was after all, was a god of Olympus. He was powerful and wise and also had a temper as do so many fathers. But he held his with Persæus and even laughed with him; he seemed to be a good father and that was all he could ask of him.

Persæus went to his mother immediately and told her as much as he could remember of the conversation. He could see the worry in her eyes as he told her of the thing he would become and how Zeus had assured him that he would be the one to determine his path. It would be interesting at the very least from the temper he had and how he sometimes responded to those that dared to push their luck with him. He only hoped he could be the man he had always expected to be; the one his mother wanted him to be. Now, at least, he had an idea what to expect and to embrace his destiny whatever that might be. He had an amusing thought wondering how inebriation would affect his expected alter ego. Now there was a mental picture he was going to find fun to explore; maybe.

Danaë helped him to put the meat in the freezer and he set to work making their dinner as promised. He couldn't help but to imagine himself as the creature he was expecting to become. Zeus had not confided in him the form he might take, although he had implied, but he thought he might know from the stories his uncles on Seriphos had related to him when he was a young boy. In his reverie he considered so many things as he sautéed the vegetables, as the potatoes boiled, the steaks were frying next to the vegetables to make use of the butter in the pan and a little salt and pepper, dinner was nearly ready. He served the piping hot meal for them both and gave thanks to Zeus for the wonderful fair and once again the very rare visit. A burgundy wine to compliment the strong taste of the venison and the meal was complete. He actually enjoyed cooking, the cleanup, not so much, but it was fulfilling to him be able to create a tasty dish that pleased even his mother's refined pallet. She was, after all, the daughter of royalty and accustomed to fine dining.

When they had made short work of the meal Persæus helped his mother clean up and then finished loading the venison into the freezer. It had been a very good weekend; the kind one remembers for a lifetime. The hunt, the comradery, the homecoming, a visit from his father, a wonderful talk and meal with his mother and the revelation of his passage into manhood. At least now he could better understand the rumblings and emotions along with the slight change in his body and spirit at times of stress that seemed to plague him from deep within. It made much more sense and he felt an elation of expectation that he'd not had before. It was a complete change in his outlook and he was feeling truly positive about it. There was a knock at the door.

It was Achilles and he looked somehow strange and anticipatory.

"May I come in?"

"Of course. Have you eaten?"

"No, I've been at the shop since we got back, it was broken into and ravaged."

"NO! Why didn't you call?"

"There's nothing that can be done tonight."

"Come in, Mother and I just finish eating, I can rewarm the food that was left over and you are welcome to sit here at the table and tell me what happened."

"That's very gracious of you, thank you."

"There isn't much to tell really, a skylight was broken out and someone used a rope to lower themselves down and open the door; I assume for others. Several tools were stolen, a few machines vandalized and the office was torn apart seemingly more for malice than anything else."

"I'm sure you called the police?"

"Yes, they seem to think it was a disgruntled employee situation as it was more to create problems than to obtain anything. At least, they claim, that's their experience in that type of thing."

Danaë came in upon hearing the conversation.

"Hello, Achilles. I'm so sorry to hear what happened, I couldn't help but overhear your conversation."

"It's not a problem Auntie, it's just one of those things that can happen."

"Do you have any idea who it could have been?" inquired Danaë.

"I have not fired anyone in years and I don't know anyone that works for me that is unhappy; so, the simple answer is no."

"Do you think," asked Persæus, "it will disturb production?"

"It will slow things a bit, but only temporarily. Some of the metal working machines are missing parts and have cut electrical cords, mostly a nuisance than anything. It will cost us a day to repair and replace what we need."

"What a terrible thing for someone to do," interjected Danaë.

Persæus mused, "Another shop, possibly?"

"That is what I'm wondering, cousin. There's no way of knowing and I'm not going to waste my time canvasing the other places for our missing tools. Financially, we are better off just buying what we need and repairing the damage rather than wasting time over investigating. We will be up and running in a day or two and we can forget about it. I am contacting Niccoli tomorrow to have grills placed under the sky lights so that can't happen again."

"Why can't we just do that ourselves?"

"We will be busy repairing and catching up on our scheduled work. Besides, Niccoli could use the business anyway."

"You are a kind man to think of Niccoli in your own time of trouble," commented Danaë.

"He is a good man and has always been there for me and never let me down. I like helping my friends when I can."

"I'm going to put Joseph in charge of most of the repairs tomorrow, I'd like you to help facilitate the work. I'll instruct the others to follow the two of you. It might not even be a full day of work but maybe we can start back at regular business by tomorrow evening."

"Certainly. Oh! By the way! Zeus stopped in, that sounds funny, more like, popped in and spoke with me."

"He sure has been poking his nose in a lot lately."

"Right? He even said hello to mother. He mentioned you and said you are

a sound and good man."

"What? No, he didn't."

"He most certainly did!"

"Well, that's unexpected. What else did he say that's out of character?"

"He spoke to me about my… condition."

"You mean the nervous tics, the barking like a dog and the cursing?" he was only kidding. "Seriously, I hope it was good news?"

"It gave me peace, for the most part. In essence, he said that I am a shape shifter and that I have the gifts of the Nephilim and the Lycanthropes. It sounds a bit ominous but he said I would learn to control them."

"Hmmm, it sounds as though there is a learning process involved. After we get through with this little hiccup at The Works, I think we should probably build a dog house for you in that corner where we always throw the scrap metal. Rather a cage."

"What do you mean, a cage?"

"Yes, why is that?" piped in Danaë.

"You may not have seen the things that I have seen of Lycanthropy and the tales of the Nephilim are enough to worry anyone. If there is a learning curve for control of the your "gifts," we might need to sequester you on occasion."

"Wouldn't that just be a bowl of cherries?"

"More like a howling good time. It beats the hangman's rope. Not that anyone could kill a Nephilim, but it's better to avoid any potential problems."

"Do you really think it's that serious?" questioned Danaë.

"I wouldn't suggest such an extreme measure unless I thought it was deadly serious."

"You do have more experience in such things compared to mother and myself. I suppose we should respect that."

"It's just precautionary but it could be well worth the trouble and expense of a good strong area to detain you during your time of transition."

Persæus and Danaë both agreed and Danaë went to clear away the dishes from the table.

"I suppose I should get out of your hair. Thanks for a fine dinner and wine; allowing me some comfort under the circumstances. I'll see you tomorrow, Persæus. We'll look at cleaning up that corner as a secondary project tomorrow; for your dog house," as he winked at Persæus.

"Thanks, cousin," Persæus said wryly, "I knew I could count on your support."

The three smiled as Achilles rose and let himself out of the door.

Regardless of the bad news of the break in and vandalism, it had been a pleasant time as it aways was when Achilles visited. They both wished they'd have seen more of him over the years but they were truly grateful for this opportunity to be family again.

Persæus and Danaë discussed Achilles proposition of a cage at the shop and determined it would be best to take advantage of the idea. Achilles could tell the other men that Persæus would be the guard at night saving the company money and ensuring there would be no further loss of time or business. That would make a good cover story for his staying in the room instead of going home at night. If the problem of the shape shifting didn't interfere with life to any great degree Achilles could hire an actual armed guard if he wished and no one would be the wiser. At this point it was only a plan and they could work out the logistics as they went. It was soon time to call it an evening and Persæus really needed a shower after the day's activities. He needed to get up early to be at the shop before most everyone else and determine a course for the work in the morning. He wanted to get to sleep early if his racing mind would allow it. The things Zeus had revealed were somewhat worrisome but he was also excited. A shape shifter; wouldn't that be a kick in the pants on Halloween?

CHAPTER FOUR:
THE CLEANUP
AND THE CAGE

After the course of the preceding day Persæus was surprisingly of sound mind and well rested and ready to face the new challenges brought by fate. He had a slice of buttered bread, some eggs and coffee with his mother that morning and spoke to her of the building plans he had in his mind for his cage. Of course, he would defer to Achillies as it would be his experience and his expense to build such a room. But he had some ideas based upon the warnings of his uncles and Achilles warning yesterday about the Nephilim. He excitedly told his mother about how he felt a concrete structure was in order and that the internal structure of the concrete walls and ceiling would require plenty of steel. The door should be steel with a steel frame with braces embedded in the walls and too small for most men much less a Nephilim. No regular door could hold him back now, it would require something special to keep him in check if he was out of control huge. Danaë admonished him that these must remain just ideas and he would need to concentrate on getting the shop back up and running before pursuing any plans for his special room. He knew, of course, that she was right and that he needed to keep his mind focused on the work of getting the shop repaired and running again.

It was nice that they lived so very close to Achilles business and he could walk to work in under ten minutes. Even if it was raining or cold it was not a bad trek and he could run that short distance if he wanted. It was good to be young and athletic but it gave pause to wonder how he would feel as he aged. To hell with that, he would just refuse to age. Well, maybe not, but hey, it worked for Zeus. Of course, Achilles was there before anyone else but Persæus was close behind and he was surprised by what he saw and that Achilles had been able to remain calm over the devastation. It seemed worse to Persæus than what Achilles had related but at least it wasn't a total disaster. Machines were smashed and tools strewn everywhere, supplies all over everything like an errant child had thrown a tantrum. Walking into the mess raised such incredible ire it was difficult to remain level headed. It made Persæus want to throttle someone.

Achilles asked Persæus to begin disassembling several of the larger welders that needed repair. They would have to look at the internals and be sure they were not compromised. He wanted Persæus to beat out the covers to make them at least presentable and to ensure they were not impinging on the internal coils. Persæus grabbed a couple of the newly arriving men to help him with that task and Joseph started to inventory the missing tools. Achilles was writing down the models and parts to fix the welders and machines with obvious external damage. Switches, power selector knobs and cable plugs would be needed on many if not most of the machines.

Some of the other men arrived and walked in with mouths agape not expecting the small disaster that slapped them in the face. Niccoli arrived soon and Achilles took him aside to peruse the sky lights and determine the best repair and grill style to cover the underside adequately. It had not rained in the past several days so they at least didn't have to deal with the mess that could have been. Niccoli felt he could fix the one broken skylight that day but the grills would take two to three days to prepare and install. Achilles was good with that. Achilles gathered everyone together and asked them to just pitch in where ever Joseph and

Persæus might need them and everyone understood it was not a matter of who was in charge but simply that someone had to coordinate things.

Joseph had the inventory done in a half hour as every tool had a place or bin assigned or marked out on the wall to keep track of them all. He had already gathered the strewn tools and replaced them on their appropriate spot so that he could make an accounting of them. Achilles had a list of external parts to repair all of the machines and Persæus and his men already had checked the internal parts on all the welders to find they had most all survived, they just looked bad externally. Several needed amperage selectors, switches and such but that was the extent of the real damage. Achilles left the men to their own and went to buy the parts to get everything up and running; if they were available. It was disheartening to walk into the mess but it was surprisingly quick to get it all straightened out and get things at least somewhat operational again. By lunch they were able to start some of their scheduled work and the rest of the men helped continue the recovery process.

The police stopped in wanting to speak with Achilles again, but he was still out trying to procure the necessary repair parts. The officers said they'd call later to see if he was in. After lunch Persæus and Joseph straightened out the mess in the office which looked as though someone was trying to make life difficult. There was nothing in there for anyone to see or steal. They did the best they could as they didn't really know what Achilles would be expecting but it at least looked better and somewhat organized. Presentable should a customer walk in.

Achilles finally made an appearance around two in the afternoon carrying several small boxes and was followed in by a delivery truck from the local supply depot. He hadn't been able to find everything but he put a good dent in the list and the men continued the necessary repairs and stocking back the replacement tools. By evening they had the shop rolling near full speed again and Achilles couldn't have been happier. Niccoli arrived with the first of the skylight grates in order to test fit it to confirm the rest could be built in like manner. He borrowed Achilles man lift and sent two of his men up to put it on the current subject of curiosity. This one was good and he promised Achilles he could have the rest done over the next two days.

Persæus started cleaning out the corner of the shop that Achilles had suggested they build his special room for his special little self. Achilles had been wanting to recycle the scrap metal for some time and did some of it on occasion as he was forced to do so by limited space. But everyone has a junk drawer and this was his. On the supply truck were two metal bins they used a fork truck to lift down and put next to the scrap pile for Persæus and the men to put the metal into. Some of it was quite dense and would bring a good price for scrap. It didn't take long and they backed in the flat bed they'd use for hunting and removed the rails from it so they could load the bins. They strapped them down so they were ready to be hauled out in the morning.

Once the corner was clear, Persæus and Achilles measured off an area four by four meters and used a chalk line to snap the outline of a room on the floor. They would start building the room once they'd caught up on the production they'd lost today; probably by the weekend. Things were starting to look good and Achilles broke out a bottle of almond liquor for the men to enjoy before heading home for the day. It had been a day of hard and frustrating work to drudge through and they'd done a stellar job of getting as much done as possible. It was good for them to pull together like this in the face of disillusionment not only to overcome adversity but also to bond for the common cause of their own financial stability.

Persæus inquired, "Achilles, would you care to chat for just a few moments about the room?"
"Sure, let's go in the office. Wow, look at this! You guys did a bang-up job in here. Thank you! What did you have in mind?"

Achilles poured a couple of double shots of a local liquor called Ouzo for themselves while they chatted in the office.

"Well, you may know better than me but I wanted to suggest a few things if that's alright?"

"Certainly. What did you have in mind?"

"From what Zeus inferred, I may grow to a much greater size during my transformation and the increased bulk and strength have me concerned."

"You should be. You will be quite formidable from what I know of both the Nephilim and the Lycanthropes."

"I was thinking a small door on the inside, something barely large enough for me to go through as a man much less a beast. Just a half meter wide and only two meters tall. I know that will cause some eyebrows to raise but it sems any advantage we have at securing me until I'm in full control might be a reasonable thing. A full size outside door to make it look right wouldn't even need to be overly strong as long as the inside door would be strong. I think we should consider this a vault and call it such to hide its true purpose; what do you think?"

"I think you're on the right track, I would still go with a secure outside door, maybe something with bars hidden within a wood casing. I can't stress enough the power I expect you to have. Zeus calls this a gift and I hope that it is, but my imagination goes crazy when I think of what I know of these two phantasms. I've already put in an order for one inch rebar for the walls and ceiling. I've got my engineer drawing up plans for a room six meters tall and a commode made of steel. I didn't think you were going to be this expensive when I hired you on, cousin!"

"I'm truly sorry for my father's inclinations but hopefully I will be valuable enough to you sometime in the future to make up for it."

"Oh, you'll pay me in blood if needed, but I'm sure it will be worthwhile in the long run. We can put the larger door on the outside and a short hall to the smaller door on the inside. We can install the smaller door after the larger one so that no one will even know it exists. The assembly will be in a corner for added strength in case your alter ego gets any desire to force the issue."

"I think we have a good plan; I feel better just having spoken with you about it."

"That's why I'm here, to make your wildest imaginings a reality. Let's just be sure to do this right. I want only the best for you, Persæus. I wouldn't want to let Auntie Danaë down either."

"Thank you, Achilles, you are the paramount example of what family is for."

"Let's get out of here so we can be fresh for tomorrow."

The men left and Achilles seemed to be in a good mood after what was accomplished in a single day. It would be good to put this little incident behind them and get caught up on the schedule. It looked like they might get a bit of rain that evening and they were both glad that Niccoli was able to jump right on that sky light. They parted ways at the intersection, each to their own home and said their goodbyes. It was a good day and a nice evening. The liquor had Persæus in a relaxed mood and he was looking forward to telling his mother of all they'd accomplished that day and the plans for the vault.

They'd caught up on the schedule and the rebar for the vault had arrived a day early so Achilles laid out the plans his engineer had drawn up for the men to study. They would first be drilling holes in the concrete floor to provide a solid and secure connection such that the walls could not be moved even if a truck crashed into them. The plans called out fifteen centimeters in depth for the holes but Achilles insisted they drill down 30 centimeters. He just knew it would be a good bet that type of strength would be necessary. They placed the holes only a foot apart and two rows six inches apart in a zig zag pattern. It was the strongest manner in which to use the steel and dynamite wouldn't touch it if they did it right. Using the cover story of a vault quashed any question of the purpose of the room and nobody questioned the extreme build. While the men drilled holes below and placed the six-meter-long rebar, others were tying cross bars up the lengths to keep them all supported and straight.

Others were building the inside form for the concrete to which they were attaching the structure. It was all very well-orchestrated and two walls were nearly complete by the lunch break. These men could really do impressive work. By evening they were beginning the columns for the ceiling supports; four larger, one at each corner and one smaller every meter in between. The columns were to the outside of the wall to leave the inside surface smooth to avoid injury if Persæus got rambunctious in his transformed self. They had to stay on schedule so Achilles allowed those that wanted the overtime to work the following day, a Sunday, if they chose and most of them did not pass up that opportunity. By three o'clock Sunday afternoon they were to a point they could bring in the pumper truck to pour the walls and columns on Monday. It was truly amazing what they had accomplished. Achilles again broke out a small bottle of liquor as a reward; as though the overtime wasn't enough, but these men had earned every bit of it and the point was not lost on Achilles or Persæus.

The pumper truck arrived first thing Monday morning and it took almost all day to fill the forms; there was a second truck waiting at all times throughout the day and as one pulled out the other entered. It really slowed production as the vault was at the back of the shop. The men had to work in cramped conditions every time a truck moved in or out but nobody complained as they felt a certain pride at what they were building. The size and strength of the vault was truly impressive and they all couldn't wait to tear off the forms to see their finished product. That would be at least a week and the engineers estimate was ten days. Even so, it would be two weeks after that for the concrete to fully cure before they could pour the beams over each of the walls and the cross beams for the ceiling. The structure was precariously close to the roof of the building and there was little room to move up top. Still, they could use at least some of the space closer to the edge for storage of smaller items and materials. It was just a bit difficult to get the hose for the pumper truck to the back wall, but they managed.

By the time the day was through, nobody wanted to leave. They cleaned up spilled concrete and swept out the dirt and tire tracks from the trucks before Achilles had to nearly chase them from the building. He chided them saying they just wanted more of his liquor. But everyone was tired in spite of the trucks doing most of the work and it had been a job well done this day. Niccoli had completed his job and had the grills up on the skylights before the trucks tied up the floor space. The whole project had come together far better and faster than expected. Now they waited for the concrete to set and cure for the next three weeks. That was the hard part, but once the forms came off in ten days Achilles had the men cut a small pass-through door in one wall for deposits; or so he said. It was really a door for food and water but after all, it was a vault and it needed access to make deposits; so the story went.

At that point they had to concentrate on the work for the shop but Achilles promised the men they could work the weekend if they wished to build the rebar trusses and forms for the ceiling. They weren't as exuberant about another seven-day week this time but nearly everyone accepted the offer as extra money was always welcome. They knew there would be no work the following weekend as they still were waiting for the concrete to cure. The walls were a foot thick and it would take every bit of time allotted by the engineer. They could relax and enjoy their families once the trusses were ready to pour. Achilles asked Niccoli to build the door for the vault and when he specified it should be covered on the outside by finely finished mahogany Niccoli had questions. Achilles simply told him that he didn't want it to look like the vault that it was.

Work continued and the vault was finished on schedule with all the accoutrements planned including the steel commode. That raised some eyebrows for the men but at this point Achilles was running out of excuses and simply said it was just in case… A very odd response but it was an answer and the guys just shrugged it off. Persæus was feeling uncomfortable about the internal feelings he was having and expressed this to Achilles.

"Do you feel like you are getting close to your time?"

"That is my fear, I'm feeling anxious and perturbed. I get upset more easily and I have a desire for the hunt that's stronger than I've ever felt; It's a very disturbing condition for me. I wish I could explain it better, but that's all I have."

"That's enough for me, we will push to complete the vault within the month. I can have Niccoli have his men build the inside door you suggested. That's going to raise some eyebrows but I can just tell the guys it's going to have some special features that no one needs to know about and I'm going to kill Niccoli and his men afterwords."

"You're kidding, right?"

"No, that's what I will say; it's not what I'll do. Just don't tell anyone, I'll keep them guessing," Achilles said with a smile.

"You dirty dog."

"Yes, but you love me anyway; and remember, you're the one becoming a dog."

Persæus gave Achilles a playful slug to the shoulder and laughed, "That's too true, cousin."

"Heel boy, roll over, play dead."

They laughed as Persæus chased Achilles around the shop barking and howling, close on his heals.

Niccoli was very happy to have more work from Achilles but was quite curious about the size of the inner doorway. Achilles just said it was to make it hard to move anything valuable in or out of the vault. No sense making it too easy for a burglar to steal him blind. Niccoli wasn't going to argue the point, after all, it made a sort of sense that he couldn't argue even as unique as was the concept. The passage between the inner and outer doors was a short one meter long and that didn't detract terribly from the space inside the vault. It was enough room for even a man as large as Persæus to walk in, close the outer door and move through the inner doorway. Persæus commented to Achilles that he didn't want to get caught in the passage while transforming; that could be deadly although, neither knew if he could die in his altered state. Another feature that drew a bit of attention were the locks on both the inside and the outside of the outer door. Achilles excuse for such a feature was to avoid being disturbed when he had to conduct business inside. That explanation seemed acceptable to everyone that asked.

Finally, the day came the vault was finished and everyone was curious what Achilles had that was so valuable to need to put inside of the structure. Again, Achilles avoided the queries of people too curious for anyone's good and simply said, "For me to know and you to find out."
Regardless, they were all proud of the work they had accomplished and still kept up with their regularly scheduled work. But it was, none the less, good to see the project finished and looking like such a monolith. Even a few friendly passersby had stopped in to peruse the vault and had been very curious about the one-off features of the structure.

Persæus was especially happy about the completion of the vault as although his eighteenth birthday was still several months out, he could feel the changes within becoming stronger and more urgent. He determined that he should sleep nights there when the moon became full as he could feel the draw of the full moon more and more because of his expected lycanthropy. Even Zeus spoke to he and Achilles on this point one evening when it was just the three of them. Achilles had not seen Zeus in the flesh, so to speak, since Zeus had saved him from death many centuries before, and he was shocked to see him now.

"I'm truly proud of you boys today."
It was shocking as he had not announced his presence as he

usually did.

"Thank you, father."

"Yes, thank you, your majesty!"

"You can drop the, your majesty, Achilles. I'm not so formal anymore. It gets in the way of real and honest discussion. Just don't forget who I am and you can address me as Zeus."

"Thank you, your majesty… Zeus."

"Thank you! I appreciate that you have taken care of my son in this matter. I knew you would come in handy someday. I also know it has been a drain on your wealth to deal with this and I will bless you with a good deal of work to help make up for it. Your men will appreciate it as well, I'm sure."

"I'm sure as well," said Achilles.

"Thank you, father."

"Remember this if someday you find yourself angry with Achilles, He has really gone above and beyond for you, son."

"I know, father."

"Hmmm, not yet, but you will very soon. I can feel your change is upon you. A bit sooner than expected but the human part of you can be a bit unpredictable, even for me. Something to do with that free will thing the Christians tend to brag about."

"Will it be painful, father?"

"I should think it will be at first. You'll be going through a second puberty in a fashion and it's going to feel strange at the very least."

"The full moon is almost upon us, are we right in assuming that might be my bane?"

"You see, I told you that you were showing wisdom. I would admonish you to be in this vault of yours before the moon rises in a few nights. Be well fed and take some salted venison and water in with you for sustenance."

Achilles had stood silent through the exchange but asked, "What can I do to help, Zeus?"

"Just be there for him, I will bless you greatly if you can just keep him through this time. He needs you and your moral support. Be the friend you would want him to be for you."

"I can do that for my cousin, Zeus."

"I can see that by what you have done already and how he adores you. Thank you both for being the men I have expected you to become."

And with that, Zeus was gone again.

Achilles waved at the empty air, "Good to see you Zeus!"

Followed by Persæus, "Ya, Thanks for dropping in, again, dad!"

A tiny bolt of lightning struck the floor in front of them with a cloud of smoke like a magician's trick and they both burst out laughing. They could hear Zeus in their minds, "Smart ass kids. Next time I might not miss."

They heard him laugh now and the laughter faded as he seemed to move away. Zeus had mellowed so much with age that the two of them really liked him and although they respected him, they were no longer afraid. They considered him as a father of adult children should be considered, a friend and a leader to be respected, but also someone to whom they could relate so much more than he once had been.

Achilles suggested Persæus bring in some supplies over the next couple of days and just put them into the vault in a corner and some more in Achilles office to be sure he had enough. Just be sure the men didn't see him put anything in the vault or it might raise questions. Persæus heart was racing a bit after their talk with Zeus and he could feel emotions and anxiety welling up inside him. He knew instinctively this was the culmination of his consummation and that life would change inexorably in the next few days. He wasn't sure he was prepared but he realized he had no choice in the matter and he must resolve himself to accept it; he must be ready as he could be under the circumstances.

They left the shop and said their goodbyes at the intersection as they might normally. Persæus was actually a bit excited to tell his mother that Zeus had visited him again. As he burst in through the front door, he found his mother entranced in the living room as shimmering around her was a golden rain with flecks piling up on the floor surrounding her. Like a child that has accidentally walked in on his parents he turned away in embarrassment having been told the story of his own conception. He waited outside for a few moments until his mother opened the door to let him come in. He was red in the face as she was also and they moved into the kitchen in embarrassed silence. Danaë spoke first and assured Pereus it was nothing about which they needed to be concerned as she placed a plate of food in front of him.

Persæus made light of the moment and simply commented, "I see I'm not the only one with news of Zeus?"
They both laughed nervously and Danaë said, "He wanted to let me know he had stopped in to speak with you and Achilles."
"Among other things…"
"Yes, among other things," she laughed. "He told me this is your coming-of-age moon cycle and that you may be a bit removed after your first change. That I should just accept whatever comes and know that you love me regardless."
"I will always love you regardless, mother."
"I know. I'm ready for whatever may come and I hope that you are too."
"It is just that I have never felt much fear and it's frightening not knowing what to expect before my first transformation and whether or not I'll have any control at all."
"I will be there that evening and maybe Achilles will stay also. We will do whatever is possible to reassure you and keep you comfortable, if we can."

It seemed the few days until the full moon flew by but with each passing day Persæus could feel the change in the pit of his stomach and the bile rising in his throat. He completed his day's work but all who knew him questioned his health that last day as he was obviously sick and he appeared to be weakening as the day progressed. Achilles finally pulled him into the office for the last half hour of the day without explanation to anyone else. Persæus couldn't express how grateful he felt for that charity. Danaë appeared unannounced in the shop but everyone knew who this beautiful woman was and she was greeted enthusiastically by all the men. In her normal grace she accepted the attention but walked briskly back to Achilles' office when she didn't see Persæus.

The three of them sat there in relative silence until the crew had gone home for the evening. Danaë pulled a loaf of bread and some wrapped meat from her bag and proceeded to make sandwiches for both men. Persæus had to check the bag to be sure it wasn't magic somehow holding all those contents. He was just playing, of course, and trying to keep his spirits up while he worried in the back of his mind of how the night would progress. Achilles brought out a bottle of desert liquor of a minty nature hoping it might relax Persæus and the mint calm his stomach.

It was well accepted even by Danaë and the three waited for the sun to begin to go down. It wasn't long and it was time for Persæus to put himself into the vault. The three walked to the large door together and Persæus hugged them both before entering. He passed through the large door; shut it and they could hear him lock it from the inside. Achilles locked it from the outside. And Persæus squeezed himself through the inside door just large enough for a man of his proportions to get inside. Achilles opened the depository pass through and let Persæus know he was locking that as well. At this point, all Achilles and Danaë could do was wait and they went back to the office where another drink was poured for them both. They heard Zeus speak in their minds and were slightly startled as they didn't expect him to be there.

"I can't be right there right now as there is business to which I must attend, but I'll be listening and will be available to Persæus if he needs me."

"Thank you, Zeus," they said in unison.

It seemed uncommon attention from Zeus but it was Persæus coming of age. But it seemed heartfelt and it was appreciated. Now they waited.

A third and fourth drink were consumed while the sun darkened and as the evening cooled. They had not noticed on the previous nights when the waxing moon was rising but they knew it would be early as it had lit up the streets well. When it did, they were sound asleep in the office from the desert liquor and the resultant sugar crash inherent with such drinks. They wakened to the most horrific howl they had never heard before as Persæus threw himself against a wall in the vault. The impact was horrendous and it shook dust from the lights hanging from the ceiling; only slightly as the room was so well fortified but, enough they knew he was something other than the loving man that had walked into the vault. That scenario continued for an hour as they sat there wondering when it would finally end… But it did end. Then it started again and they realized that a cloud had crossed in front of the moon but now had receded again.

It was nigh onto midnight when the monster within finally subsided with its rampage and the two caretakers finally felt they could relax. Achilles was beside himself with curiosity and went to the deposit door to look in. When he did, he realized his mistake as two large eyes and horrible dog breath greeted him and the tirade started all over again. It was insanity for another three hours and Achilles and Danaë couldn't believe the monster was still awake. But finally, it ended and it seemed it was over for the night so Achilles again checked the deposit door. He saw the creature laying on the floor breathing gently. He couldn't believe the size of the monster and he was surprised to notice it had wings that were wrapped around it as though to keep it warm. They were wise to build the room six meters tall as Persæus was at least three meters in his transformed body. He was indeed a giant as the Nephilim were reputed to be.

He called Danaë over to look in and she breathed in a sharp breath of shock and horror when she saw what her son had become. She immediately called upon Zeus insisting he appear before her; she was met with only silence but she felt his presence. She knew he was watching and was satisfied that the coward wouldn't show himself.

"I heard that, woman. There is nothing I can do so there is no need for me to be involved. I'm glad you are there for him and I am keeping up with his progress. Just stop with the name calling, it's a good thing I like you."

She just smiled; she knew he couldn't resist when she demeaned his godhood.

"Ya, you think you know me."

But she did know him and they both knew it.

Danaë and Achilles retired to the office and had another desert liquor to calm themselves and to celebrate the monster having passed into slumber. Achilles set the alarm on his phone to wake them before the men came in, it would be a short night for them both but hey had to get Persæus up and out before the crew started arriving; that is, if he was again human. The minty liquor did its job and they both fell asleep just in time for the alarm to waken them. "Isn't that just how a sleepless night goes?" they both expressed to each other. They checked the deposit window and to their great relief, Persæus was indeed human again, dressed and waiting for them to release him.

"I can't believe I was so worried about this thing. It was a breeze! I fell asleep and wakened naked and that was all there was to it! My shoulders are a bit sore from sleeping on the concrete but I feel great!"

"You should have seen it from our point of view," said Achilles. Danaë nodding her head in agreement. That's when Persæus noticed that they looked like crap warmed over and asked them what it was he was missing. So, they described their night and he sat in wonderment not knowing if he should believe them. It certainly explained why he wakened naked and his shoulders were sore. He was ravenous and had at some point eaten all the salted venison in the vault so they broke out the food still in Achilles office and had a make shift breakfast before they expected the crew to come in. Persæus re-entered the vault and swept it out as contrary to what the comics and movies showed, the fur and nails did not simply shrink back into the body. He had shed them and they lay scattered about the floor and the mess needed to be cleaned up.

Danaë kissed Persæus and hugged him and hugged Achilles also before excusing herself to go home for the morning. She would try and get some sleep somewhere in between the household chores. She also had to clean up what was left of the gold that had not swept up well when Zeus had showered her and stash that with the rest for use later; she would likely convert it into their bank account and give the banker something over which to wonder. There was a myriad of questions the first time they made a deposit, she could imagine the questions this time. If he only knew that she was consort to a high god of Olympus. She smiled at that as it wasn't so much funny as she felt it an honor that he, in some fashion of his own, loved her and their son.

It was a day like any other day when production began and Persæus could not believe his level of energy as he did twice the work of any man in the shop. He had always been a strong and productive employee at whatever he set his mind on, but he was surprised at what he was able to do today. So was everyone around him, "Persæus, slow down, you're making us look bad," the men would say. He did his best but he was so energized by his knew found strength that he found it not as simple as what one might expect. He was a dynamo and was enjoying it but to keep the peace, he tried to let the others keep up with him. By noon they had gotten most of the work for the day done and Achilles gave them the choice of going home when they finished or they could continue into the next day's schedule and probably have an extra day off over the weekend. The guys chose the long weekend. The fishing was good right now and many wanted to help their extended families with the boats and nets. That was something Achilles had always admired about these humans, was their love of family and community.

When the evening approached, Danaë returned with more food in a basket so they could enjoy the night as much as possible with sustenance in their tummies. She even brought a bottle of wine for the meal and the three of them sat down and gave thanks after the men had gone home. As the sun began to go down, Persæus could feel the change coming on this time, as though there was a warning sequence of which he'd not been aware previously. He felt butterflies in his stomach and a sense of his skin tingling, a slight ache in his fingernails and his bones felt reminiscent of the growing pains of youth.

He entered the vault early as he was concerned the moon might appear earlier than they were expecting. This time he removed his clothing and left it in the entry passage after closing and locking the outside door as he didn't want to ruin another set of clothing upon his transformation. It was not long before he was back to the scenario of trying to ram his way through the walls and howling in frustration but tonight, to those waiting outside, it seemed as though his effort was not as intense. As though his monster from within was realizing this would not work, that possibly there was some semblance of intellect to the creature. Achilles opened the deposit door again tonight and again the creature was looking back at him. This time it did not elicit a response as the Persæus monster seemed to recognize Achilles whether from the night before or as his long-known cousin. And indeed, he rested his fury self after that and earlier than he had the night before for which Achilles and Danaë were grateful. At least this night, although the office chairs were much less than comfortable, they might get a little sleep. They poured a night cap and were out before they had finished it.

The night passed quickly and soon the two caretakers heard Persæus knocking on the outer door to be released shortly before the sun came up. They knew for a fact he had returned to his human form as there was no way a creature of that magnitude could have squeezed into the passage to knock on the door. This morning Persæus thanked them and after sweeping out his sheddings, sat and told them that he had been aware of things that night. Not as in reality but as in a dream. It was a strange, in between feeling that he was in a place of exploration and discovery. He had realized that he had wings and had spread and folded them several times. He'd had the realization that he did not have the room to fly but he could flap them and feel that they were fully able to support his great mass. He was in wonderment as to his great size and his clawed hands and he reached up to touch is long ears that heard them speaking even through these thick walls. He even smelled the hot buttered rum they had not finished and he knew they had not finished due to the odor that remained when they both started snoring.

"I don't snore!" they both claimed.

"Oh, yes. I assure you, that you both do," Persæus said with a knowing and playfully belligerent smile.

He was feeling strong and refreshed. Danaë prepared homemade bread with butter, strawberry jelly and slices of crispy bacon on the side while Achilles made a pot of his highly acrid, cup eating espresso that he dosed heavily with honey, cream and a touch of vanilla. They all felt good about Persæus progress and hoped that tonight might show more progress of this nature. The day was humid and mild in temperature due to cloud cover and no one really wanted to work but they all pushed themselves to have that long weekend of fishing with their families. Persæus was affected the least by the humidity but even he spoke up for an extra break that afternoon so they could all rest and cool down. As the day passed it was obvious they would finish the schedule early and they would have their long weekend; everyone slowed just a bit. One of the men had started a home business of making his own brand of wine and had brought some of it in. Achilles gave the go ahead and they enjoyed the product of their brother's efforts. It was quite good with an aftertaste of maple and peach and they complimented him on his skill as a vintner.

This was the third and final night of the completely full moon and Persæus was looking forward to what might be, as it seemed it might be a red-letter moment in his life. Again, Danaë brought in a meal for them and some wine to go with it. On top of the previous bottles the guys had imbibed Persæus and Achilles were feeling light hearted and expectations were running high. The three of them teased, joked and laughed about the various happenings of the week including Zeus being present, the lack of sleep, Persæus walking in on his mother with Zeus. A lot had happened and it was a lot to digest. But regardless of their revery and conversation the time came that Persæus had to retire to the vault, his dog house as Achilles was beginning to call it. He did so with anticipation of a positive outcome and he was light at heart for this night's end.

Achilles and Danaë again retired to the office and enjoyed a few desert shots, something with some gold flecks in it and another that was green and minty. Soon the moon had risen over the surrounding houses yet nary a peep they heard from the vault. It was silent and they became curious. Achilles opened the deposit window and again he saw the monster within staring at him. It spoke, "Dear cousin, I am well and in control." The voice was deep and gravely.
"Are you sure, Persæus?"
"Yes, cousin. I can speak, can I not? I am just different now but you know who I am. I am in control of the monster."
"Yes, I do know who you are in the daytime, but not right now. What is your purpose in speaking to me instead of trying to tear

your way out?"

"It is obvious you have built this cage to withstand even my great strength and I cannot even spread my great wings to fly, not that I could escape through the concrete and rebar anyway. Your cage for me is formidable and I compliment you on the incredible structure you built to hold me."

"We aimed to please, oh great nephilimic lycanthrope. I hope you are at least a little bit comfortable?"

"Not at all, my dear cousin. It hurts my shoulders that my great weight must be borne by them on this concrete floor as I sleep and the humidity and the close quarters make me feel claustrophobic. I do wish you could let me out."

"But how would you exit through the inner doorway? You cannot fit through such an opening!"

"Ah, but I could and you can see that I am in control," he said as he shed his fur and shrank nearly to Persæus normal size. Yet he still retained his large ears, his fangs and the claws on his hands and feet.

"Yes, I see that you are in control and I must give you credit, that is quite impressive."

At that point Danaë's curiosity had been piqued and she strode over to peak in.

"Mother! I am so happy to see you came to check on me."

"Of course I did, Persæus. That is you, isn't it?"

"Of course it is, mother. I am in control."

"You are certainly different from the past two nights, my beautiful son."

"Yes, mother. I am in control."

Achilles turned to whisper into Danaë's ear, "He keeps saying that."

"Yes, I do. Because it is true, did you not think that I would hear you?"

"I suspected, but I still wanted to gauge your response. I am not impressed."

The creature within backed up a step and snorted indignation at the statement made by Achilles, the response spoke volumes more than the creature knew.

"Such arrogance from a puny human when I am in control and knowing that I could break you if I could get to you."

"My point exactly and you reveal yourself and your intentions by your own arrogance; you are a creature not yet ready to be free."

"WHAT?! How dare you to judge me puny man child! I am in control!"

"Ah, but that's where you are wrong; my mother made me a god and I am more god than even you, creature."

"But I am in control and you must do as I require!"

"Yes, you keep telling us you are in control. Yet, you are the one in the cage and we control that," replied Achilles.

"You are not yet my son, oh creature of the night," decried Danaë. "If you are really my son Persæus, tell us your father's name and our names. You have not mentioned them and I think you are not as much the demi-god Persæus as you are the creature your father has created within you. Your awareness and control are more that of the creature than that of Persæus. Tell us our names, creature! Speak them now or stay the night in the vault."

With that the creature howled and grew to his other self, fully large and covered in hair. He rushed the deposit window with his arm outstretched as though to grab at the two caretakers through the opening but, Achilles was quick to close it and get the hasp in place before he could reach through. The lock slipped onto the hasp and although the creature tried to push it open it was in vain. They had already stepped back and he could not have reached them where they stood anyway. There was howling and growling and panting and they could hear him still try to force the deposit window from time to time but eventually the tirade ended. They had already gone back to the office to have a few more sips to calm their nerves and discuss the conversation when things finally quieted down. They knew already the creature could hear their words but they didn't hide them as they wanted it to know they understood it better than it understood what it thought were their vulnerabilities.

"Do you think he will ever return to being my son, Achilles?"

"I do believe that Zeus would not have put this upon his own child if he didn't know the final product."

"I suppose I must pray and trust that you are correct; that Zeus is wise and that Persæus is strong."

"It seemed obvious to me that the creature was speaking and not Persæus, but your test was wisdom in real time and you exposed him succinctly."

"Thank you, Achilles. I was only trying to help make the reality known if it was to be so."

"And you did a fine job of it. Thank you for that. I believe this will be primarily over tonight but we may want to secure Persæus next month as well. That creature is wise and vile and it had nothing but bad intentions tonight."

"That was so disturbingly obvious. I could hardly believe the malice that I felt from it. It truly is evil incarnate coming from within my son at this point. That was not the wonderful young man that I raised and from who I long to see the integrity and respect for others that he has always exuded."

"I do believe you will see that man return next month even when the creature is allowed to come through, it will not be allowed to influence him. I really expect Persæus will be successful in keeping the dark side of his alter ego in check."

There was a bang on the outside door of the vault but they ignored it as they knew it was just the creature looking for attention. It had apparently shrunken to near human size in order to pound on the outer door trying to startle them. And it had; they were not expecting that, but they did not feel it was wise to acknowledge the creature's effort.

They soon fell asleep and the creature made no interruptions to their dreams. When morning arrived, they knew that Persæus would be himself again and when they checked the deposit window, they were happy to see his smiling countenance dressed and waiting patiently for them to let him out. He again went straight to sweeping up his sheddings and disposed of them in the dumpster outside. He had used the inside garbage yesterday and there were questions as from where so much hair had come. They chalked it up to Mr. Nobody as that seemed to work for so many teenagers and who were they to argue with teenage logic?

"I remember everything!" he said excitedly. "I'm glad you recognized it was not me. I tried to get out and warn you but it was great to feel the creature's frustration and dismay that you figured out its ploy. He lost a great battle in his own mind last night and you helped me put him in a cage in my mind. He shouldn't be a problem anymore but both he and I heard you in the night and You are wise to lock me up again next month just in case. He's already making designs to try and take over again and we must prevent that until he loses heart. He can only do that on the full moon but if I am in control, he cannot be. We will win this battle before long and I will be able to start using my new found blessings at that point. I do feel much stronger though, I know you have noticed."
"We certainly have," said Achilles. "You have single handedly lead these men to a long weekend and You are now elevated in their minds. They respect you and you are going to have to live up to that. Just don't overstep with Joseph, he is your leadman and you need to remember that he is in charge under me."

Persæus knew he could not usurp Joseph's position and authority and he hoped he hadn't done so in any way in his exuberance and desire to complete the schedule early. He wanted nothing more than to help the men have their long weekend. He was excited to have the extra time off as well and he planned on taking his mother to the local flea market so that she could be there a day early for the best selection and deals. She enjoyed buying at the flea market and selling to the neighborhood women that couldn't get there. She only charged a pittance for her efforts and the neighborhood ladies loved her for making things available to them to which they might otherwise not have access. It was a big win for everyone. Those were the days they really felt like they were becoming part of the neighborhood and Danaë truly enjoyed having her neighbors walk away with a smile knowing they'd gotten a great deal on one thing or another. It looked like this might be an extra special weekend of small treasures for the ladies.

On the days at the flea market, they would borrow a two wheeled donkey cart from an older gentleman down the street and Persæus would be the donkey for his mother's errands. Old Cephus had asked one time why they didn't at least buy a scooter with which to pull it and Persæus extoled the virtues of getting some exercise by pulling it himself. In truth, it was that they didn't want the added expenses of repairs, fuel, insurance and registrations. Not to mention having to roll the thing through the house to put it on the back porch and tracking in all that dirt. They wouldn't leave it on the street out front for fear of damage or theft. It's not that they couldn't afford the extra expenses but this also gave them a reason to go and visit old Cephus on occasion. He was kind to let them borrow his cart and they always made a point of buying some bread, sausage and wine for him when they borrowed it.

Their haul from the flea market was especially prosperous getting there a day early and Danaë couldn't help but overload the cart with treasures the women at home would absolutely adore. There were always carpets but she was able to pick out the very best on Friday as opposed to Saturday and they were of premium quality. Many brass and silver serving trays and trinkets that drew the eye and especially quality housewares the women would be fighting over. Persæus even got involved as being early, all of the hunting, fishing and camping gear was fresh and not rummaged through and he thought it might attract the attention of the men living nearby. If not, he thought he might sell them to the guys at work. It was a very successful trip and they had offers on many of the items as they pulled in front of their home and before they were even prepared to sell them. A few of the people liked the bounty so much that there were a couple of bidding wars that occurred spontaneously and Persæus had to get between a couple of the men that wanted a lobster trap that he'd snagged.

For the most part, the month went by as any month and without incident but eventually the moon was due to rise in the night sky again. Persæus could feel his alter ego wanting a chance to make itself known again but He was beginning to wonder if he might control it without incident. It seemed much weaker this time and he could actually manifest his wings during the day as the time got close. It felt good to know that he was gaining the necessary control to keep the Nephilim wolf at bay and still manifest its power. He felt powerful and confident and telling this to his mother, she warned him not to become over confident as this was all very new to them all. She warned to err on the side of caution and he knew she was probably right. So, he bode his time even though it sorely tested his patience and he waited for the new moon to rise as it was already a three-quarter crescent.

The night of the first full moon finally arrived and the surging of power that was in Persæus was rising to a crescendo which elated him with its promise of power and flight. He couldn't help but tell Danaë and Achilles of the feelings welling up inside of him and they both prayed for him in their caution over such exuberance. No one knew what to expect of such a combination of spirits within him and they could only speculate at the outcome. Again, Danaë had brought dinner, this time some venison steaks with sautéed vegetables flat bread with honey and wine. It was a feast fit for kings and even gods, such as they were. She also brought some of the salted venison for the morning and eggs they could fry in bacon grease come morning and more flat bread if there was any leftover tonight. Both men seemed ravenously hungry and Danaë was concerned she might have to go out for more. It was almost like having a camp out but for the one obvious detractor.

Persæus could feel the rage of the monster within and chose to enter the vault early, just in case it had any surprises for him. The power of the creature was strong within him but the rage seemed separate and divorced from Persæus himself. It was different from the previous manifestations and that encouraged all of them. Regardless, he entered the vault, stripped down for the sake of his clothing and waited.

"You think you are in control, don't you Persæus?" he could hear in his head. "You are not, you are weak, you are nothing. You are but a child that thinks it can dominate and overpower that which is superior"

"Silence foul beast, you are the one that is trapped within me, you are the one that is weak. Your power is mine. You are not nothing, you are a tool, for you are now mine and I own you! You have nothing over me as your power is usurped and taken as hostage."

The monster raged within him and caused him to howl but it could not manifest itself. Persæus was right, he owned the monster and as powerful as it was it could not consume him. Persæus laughed and thought to himself, it is powerful but it deceives itself.

"I only toy with you, for I am the one in control and you are but a child with which I will play. I demean you with my presence and I kick you as you are down. You are powerless over me."

"You are but a clown and a mental patient that I keep in a strait jacket behind the bars of my mind. You are locked away in a room from which you will never escape. You don't even know where you are or how to get out. You only have the power to speak but no longer can you manifest yourself without my expressed permission. I can gag your mouth if I wish but I choose to let you demean yourself for the sake of my entertainment. You are but a jester on a stage and I can walk out anytime. I am laughing at you and you will never escape the cell in which you are a captive."

Again, the creature howled but Persæus muzzled it to make his point. Achilles and Danaë suffered themselves to look in through the deposit door because they could not believe the creature had taken Persæus this cycle. They did not believe their eyes and ears as they witnessed both sides of the conversation emanating from Persæus mouth. First the familiar voice of Persæus and then the low gravely growl of the Satan's spawn within him.

"You lie to yourself puny human, you lie to me and I only allow it such that you think you have control over me, you are nothing and no one! I am the god of your soul and you will obey me!"

"I am a demi-god; I have the power of Zeus and I will call upon him to punish you if you do not quiet your insolent mouth, beast of hell!"

The creature tried in vain to manifest itself and Persæus allowed it to grow ears and nothing more. He then laughed, "You deceive yourself oh, fury fake of a demon. You have no power except as I allow you!"

Persæus forced the ears to subside and allowed himself a wry and snide smile to cross his face to taunt the vile creature. Again, it tried to force a howl to emanate from Persæus to no avail. Persæus had the creature by the nether regions and they both knew it. He squeezed on the vile creature's sensitive parts and made it howl in his mind but not in his voice. It was in incredible pain and suffering and Persæus, being kind and not vindictive, released it laughing as to its fate. It had true hate in its heart for him at that moment. It loathed him beyond hatred. The Nephilim within him sufficed itself to just go along for the ride as it was more benign and didn't care for power but rather just longed for freedom.

"I am surprised and proud of you, son," came the familiar voice of Zeus.

"May you burn in hell!" the creature snarled at the god of Olympus.

"Oh, I have done that, you moronic creature of the night. I survived! I rose up again after three days! I now sit on high! Can you?" and Zeus laughed mockingly.

The creature cringed such that Persæus could feel it and Persæus laughed along with Zeus.

"I thought that I had to do this on my own, father?"

"But you have, can't you tell? It is defeated and without recourse. It only mocks you hoping that you will fail to realize that you have won."

"That is my earnest feeling, father. If that is the case, must I listen to its incessant babbling?"

"You may stop it whenever you choose."

"Then I so choose." And the creature was no more. It was completely gone and Persæus had no perception of its presence. He was free. "Was it really so simple?"

"Yes, son. You had it within you the entire time. You simply had to realize it. You have won."

Persæus allowed his ears, claws, wings and fangs to emerge without fear of the creature but he did not grow; and no fur... He hated the fur; he hated cleaning up that mess. The caretakers and Zeus clapped and laughed their approval as they understood his lack of fur regardless of the fact that he looked a bit ridiculous without it; like a sphynx cat. So, he allowed it to grow and they all nodded their approval. Zeus looked toward the deposit door and he and Persæus were suddenly standing on the other side next to Danaë and Achilles.

"Thank you both for taking care of Persæus through this time of hardship and trial. You have made me very happy and you have earned favor in my sight."

"Zeus," said Danaë, "In all honesty to your power and glory, we did not do it for your favor as much as we appreciate it; and we truly do appreciate it. We did it for love."

"And love is the ultimate gift and sacrifice my dear Danaë."

They invited the king of Olympus to join them in a toast to the new and improved Persæus who had now made a mess on the floor shedding his fur. To their great surprise and great joy, the god of the Greek gods accepted their invitation and they all toasted. They toasted first to Zeus in his wisdom, he thanked them, they toasted Persæus in his victory over evil, they toasted themselves for their perseverance in support of Persæus and they toasted the liquor that was giving them more reasons to toast; then they toasted to Persæus again as he covered himself in clothing. Even the god of Olympus was laughing and enjoyed the levity and conversation.

"As much as I love you all and enjoy you including me in your revelry, I must go."

And with that, Zeus was gone again. Seriously? But how could they complain? He had joined them, reveled with them, toasted with them, how many others could claim such a close relationship with the god over all other gods of Olympus? They could only laugh and celebrate such a victory and close communion with Zeus. It was a night of incredible joy and accomplishment. They had pleased the god of Olympus, stayed the beast, protected their loved one and persevered over insurmountable odds. It was a good night and it was time for them all to head for their respective homes. Zeus had kept his word and the shop had so much work it was wearing every one out. Achilles had to hire more men and tomorrow was going to be a good day.

The sun came out early these days as did the moon as Persæus, Danaë and Achilles well knew. But it was no longer a threat and they resumed life as normal with the threat of severe and all-encompassing evil no longer their concern. They all had a new lease on life and they were happy deep within their souls for the risen 'son' that survived temptation, had given them hope beyond hope that there was more to life than just worry and a life without goodness. They knew now, it was up to them to manifest the hope and righteousness needed to make life worthwhile. They knew this was within their grasp and their will. They were now in control and there was no one and nothing that could convince them otherwise. They were, in some manner, the gods of Olympus in this small Greek town and they had Zeus' ear if that was needed. They knew their part and their responsibility and they were happy to accept their part in the story. Even the Catholics and Christians might agree. It was a glorious morning.

There was an incomprehensible joy to their day and they knew that the entire world had changed overnight regardless that they could not understand the entirety of it. They were a part of something greater than the world had ever known since its inception. They were stunned and beside themselves with what could only have been described as special knowledge. They were elated but couldn't tell anyone why. It was frustrating beyond reality. Yet, in some way, they were at peace with their conflicting emotions. It was complicated. That damned Zeus; they just knew he was laughing at them. And they were right. He did have a sense of humor as he had proven so many times. After all, why make the giraffe's neck so long when he could have just made the trees shorter? Right? Such a simple fix. Zeus... Did he have a devious nature or was it just his sense of humor. Most saw it as his humor and in fact, who else would have given a platypus a duck's bill? A mammal that lays eggs? Seriously? He had to know how to laugh. But the three in the shop knew this of him. He was their father, their lover their friend.

They appreciated Zeus more than ever and they could only talk amongst themselves about their love of a being that so used and abused them to only their betterment. How could they not love him? He was not always forthright with them but he never harmed them in a manner that did not make them better. How was that possible? How could they not love him for that? So, it was that life continued for the three musketeers Persæus helping Achilles and Joseph break production records and bringing prosperity to themselves and the men that depended on them. They even had reason to use the vault as a vault for a change as Achilles wealth grew in never-before-seen proportions. Even with having given his men an unheard-of raise of 50% over the competing wage in the town.

Now everyone wanted to work for Achilles' The Works and with orders increasing almost every day they might have to hire more people. Already Danaë was helping with the paperwork and scheduling as Achilles no longer had the time to do much of it. She was asking Achilles to consider hiring someone to do it full time such that she could be an assistant instead of working full time. After all, she was consort to the god Zeus. Achilles just teased her that she was being lazy, but he was looking into her suggestion. He really was, he loved his auntie. Zeus had kept his word to bless them for protecting and helping Persæus through his time of transition and it was almost more than they could handle. But the vault was being put to good use and a heavier locking system had to be installed on the outside as it began to fill with gold and fiat currency. They'd moved in shelves and tables along with a few chairs so that the part time accountant he was going to hire could organize and keep records. Achilles had inquired about the warehouse next door where he could expand and the owner was willing to sell for a premium. At this point Achilles wasn't going to complain but he did get the price down just a bit as the insurance and taxation authority placed its value well below the asking price.

He invited Niccoli to move into the newly acquired warehouse to save on renting where he was; for which he was extremely grateful. The owner of his building, not so much but he had it rented out again in only a couple of months. It was a good match as Nicoli's shop did a lot of the smaller jobs that The Works had never done and now, they were a more rounded production team. They put up a new sign, A & N The Works; because it really was the entire works. They constructed a passage between the two warehouses such that construction materials would stay dry during inclement weather. Most of the materials were stored in the newly acquired warehouse as the smaller parts production required less space. Niccoli was now the president of small parts production and Achilles was CEO and the president in charge of large parts production. Joseph became the vice president of small parts while Persæus was the vice president of large parts. There was a little grumbling that Persæus had moved up so quickly but he was a giant among them, worked twice as hard as any of them and after all, he was the owner's cousin. And no one wanted to offend the beautiful Danaë. Regardless of his position in the company, he still worked among the men on the floor and they seemed to appreciate that fact as well. It wasn't often an executive officer worked alongside his men. And the company grew almost exponentially thanks to Zeus influence and Achilles business acumen.

The town was growing as well because of the influx of business and the growing wealth of the men that worked for A & N The Works. Many had started small businesses for their wives or relatives and everyone was prospering. The town saw more homes with fresh paint and flowerboxes under the windows, new restaurants opening and the flea market had grown along with the prospering businesses. Soon word got out that a great deal of business that used to occur in other small towns was now being conducted locally for a cheaper price and that did not sit well with some. It piqued the interests of Set and he decided that he wanted to find out what larceny had been put into play by Zeus. He walked into The Works one morning asking for the owner. It was obvious by his size, his stride, his carry and his clothing that he was an important person, at least in his own mind, and there was speculation among the men that he might want to buy the company.

Walking out to greet the visitor Achilles knew immediately who he was and was filled with trepidation knowing Set's reputation. Never the less, he greeted him cordially, "What brings you out of Egypt, Set."

"I have come to see this upstart company that has made waves as far South and East as the head waters of the Nile River."

"Oh, that cannot be! We are just a local business that has a solid customer base and a reputation for quality."

"That pays your men a premium salary with which no one can compete. You garner loyalty through high pay, fair treatment and premium working conditions. We have heard everything about you in the Egypt."

"I only treat my men as I would want to be treated. That is not a crime, last time I checked."

"But you draw all the best craftsmen from farther than the eye can see and they will not leave you no matter the provocation."

"That is a good thing for them and for me."

"But the rest of the world suffers because of it."

"The rest of the world should follow our business model."

"But we would need to give up much of our wealth and that isn't going to happen."

"Do I look like my wealth is hurting?"

"I must admit, you seem to be doing very well."

"And so, we are."

"Rumor has it that you don't keep your money in the bank."

"We don't advertise what we do with our money, it is no one else's concern."

With that, Set walked over to the vault and reached for the deposit door. Persæus had been quiet this entire time but seeing Set head for the vault, had also walked over and without an introduction or a single word, slammed the deposit door nearly taking off Set's fingers.

He allowed the monster's voice to emanate from his throat saying, "You are a guest in our business, please conduct yourself as such."

The shock on Set's face made Achilles laugh.

Set was not amused and said, "Make your dog heel, Achilles."

With that Persæus grew a couple of inches and growled allowing his eyes to glow red, something he had not done in years was allow his eyes to glow. That got Set's attention and even the men in the shop stepped back as they'd never seen Persæus in his alter ego; this was new.

"You have my apology gentlemen. I did not realize my words were spoken to so many gods."

With that, he spoke in the monster's voice, "I am Persæus, son of Zeus and you have offended me."

With that Achilles stepped up and put his hand on Persæus arm to calm him and said, "Thank you my cousin," which again caught the attention of Set. "You are much appreciated but I want no bloodshed today. Tomorrow, perhaps; but not today."

They both laughed looking directly into Set's eyes and seeing a lack of surety they knew he was done for this visit.

Achilles spoke, "Thank you for stopping in. You might announce your intent the next time so that we can prepare for guests and be more hospitable."

With that, Set turned and walked away with obvious purpose, his highborn posture somewhat reduced. He had not been prepared for the encounter and was most certainly put off by what he'd seen and heard. A few of the men that knew Persæus clapped and the rest just nodded their assent not knowing quite what to think.

"Go and visit with the men for a bit. You shocked them just as much as you did Set. Let them ask any questions they might have and answer them truthfully. You are exposed now; you may as well roll with it. Come and talk with me later."

CHAPTER FIVE: KNOWING WHEN IS PRICELESS

The men were full of questions as Achilles had suspected. And they were not afraid to ask. Persæus just smiled and assured the men that he was indeed a son of Zeus and had been blessed with some of the powers of the gods. He did not go into detail but warned them that there was much more that he would not say about his powers as the son of Zues but that they didn't need to be fearful of him as he was their friend and protector as well. They figured out that day they were indeed in the presence of greatness of which they'd not expected. Persæus was far more than any had understood and his humility and charity were far more than they'd come to expect from any god or demi-god. Persæus gave Danaë much of the credit for his charity and the men knew it to be true of his beautiful mother. She was indeed as beautiful inside as she was outside.

When the questions were done and the men went back to work from the unscheduled break, Persæus went to see Achilles in his office. Niccoli was there as were Leon and Joseph and they'd been speaking already so Persæus felt like he was late for the game. It wasn't anything huge at this point but Achilles knew much of Set and he didn't like the attention they had gotten form him. He was bad business if one was on his wrong side and it appeared that they were already, without even knowing it. If he had sailed across the Mediterranean Sea from Cairo, as Achilles suspected was his route, then they had indeed raised some eyebrows and possibly made enemies with some of the worst in the region. Cairo was a center of business for the entire Southern Mediterranean Sea And much damage could be done concerning any expansion just from that one port. Achilles wanted Niccoli to understand what was afoot even if it never affected them as the possibility was incredibly dangerous. Set was the god of chaos but he seldom set foot out of Egypt and for this to have occurred, there were probably others besides him that were interested in what was going on with the business at The Works.

Persæus suggested that he and Achilles stay the night in the two warehouses just in case there was any trouble to which Achilles agreed. He wanted, however, to have others of the men volunteer for this possibly dangerous sleep over and that they all be armed. So, a meeting was called for all the men in both warehouses and they were apprised of the situation and promised dinner, wine and a small bonus if they chose to stay the night. Many had to spend the night in their homes for various reasons but about twenty men volunteered for the duty although many of those had to go home first but promised to return. There was no reason to disbelieve any of the men, they were loyal and they all had proven their integrity on many occasions. Achilles was quite pleased with the number of men that were able to volunteer. It would be a security force with which to reckon if it became necessary.

Leon and Persæus went to a local eatery to order the dinner for twenty plus the five executives and Danaë. They made sure the place could handle the order and didn't complain when they were told it would be an hour and a half to prepare. They had sprung it on them, after all. In the meantime, Danaë purchased bread and wine for the men staying so they could satiate their hunger while waiting for the late dinner. Achilles recommended that any man that had weapons should retrieve them before the dinner arrived so they could be prepared for anything. It was an unknown situation and they had to prepare for anything. Persæus and Leon had kept their heads on a swivel as they walked to and from the eatery surveying for possible spies that might be watching their activities. Especially within a block of the shop. They were satisfied that they'd not seen any but that didn't mean they weren't there lurking in the shadows somewhere. But they didn't expect any trouble until after dark anyway. Purveyors of evil and chaos didn't like the light of day.

The dinner meal arrived in almost exactly an hour and a half and to any watching it might look like a simple feast for a group of the workers, possibly for a job well done. By that time, the sun had set and they closed the doors and locked them; no sense inviting in the possible scourge. They all hoped it would be without necessity in the end but somehow, a feeling, a pall was upon them and that is sometimes best respected. They didn't want to drink too much wine in case their wits had to be sharp but they all felt relaxed and jovial in spite of the situation and the ominous cloud that seemed to hang over them. Achilles was glad of this as he knew that the chaos that Set would bring probably would begin in their minds. They prayed to Zeus for clarity that they might be prepared for whatever might come their way. The meal and the wine made them tired after a hard day of work and as each man drifted off Achilles found himself alone except for Persæus.

"Do you find it strange that only we of Olympus are awake so early in the evening?" queried Persæus.
"I certainly do," Achilles replied as he started to shake the men to try and waken them from their slumber. They stirred but didn't waken and the two knew they had all been drugged. Achilles went to the shelves and found several bottles of ammonia they kept for cleaning certain surfaces and he started to pour them onto the floor. It made a stink of horrible proportion but the men started to waken. Oh, they did whine about the smell but it was bringing them out of their stupor. Danaë had also been

overcome but wakened from the ammonia and as she realized what had happened, she began making strong coffee that could almost dissolve a spoon and making everyone drink. Set, or his operatives, had almost succeeded in their devious plan, but the men were ready regardless of the treachery.

They encouraged half the men to hide behind material, boxes and machines while the rest were to feign their drugged condition. They left on the lights such that it would seem they had all passed out from the drugs and they waited. The perpetrators were confident in their drug as it was an hour before they heard someone prying at the doors to both warehouses. Some of the men had fallen out again but their compatriots nudged them when they heard the commotion at the doors. They laid in wait for the burglars to make their entrance and when they did, it was only a party of ten to the twenty-six that awaited them inside. It was over before it even started as the men in hiding came in behind the burglars and the men waiting around the food and wine simply stood with swords, bows and even a few pistols at the ready. The burglars had been made fools and the only unfortunate result was that Set as not with them. The reception team beat the story from them within minutes and they knew it was Set that was in charge. They called the police and the perpetrators were bound and gagged and held until they arrived. The police weren't sure what to do with so many as Phthia was not really an active town, but they loaded them into a panel truck and carted them off to jail.

Danaë was the one that was suspicious of the burglars and mentioned that she didn't think they were the real raiding party. The men stood in stunned silence as it soaked in that maybe she was right. Wouldn't it fit that they were to believe they had beaten Set's plan and then go home for the night leaving the shops unguarded? They reset the plan and asked the police to leave two men with radios with them for a few hours. The captain balked because he had only four men, but he could see they were probably right and agreed to leave the men with them. This time they shut the doors and turned out the lights as though they had all gone home. They couldn't lock the doors because of the damage the first crew had done but if they were right, it wouldn't matter. Another half hour passed and sure as the day is long the doors rose and in came a gang of five men along with Set. Set was in his full godly glory tall and shimmering and looking for trouble and Persæus was the one to bring it to him. When the lights came up Set was not prepared for a Werewolf of three meters with wings spread and fangs dripping saliva. Set's men seeing the host before them fled and even the men of The Works coward in fear at the sight of Persæus. With his claws and fangs and eyes glowing red. He was indeed an awful sight and he knew it! Even Chaos could not steel himself against the manifestation of the demi-god that stood before him and he coward on his knees.

"Just as Horus defeated you after eighty years of battle, tonight, my son Persæus defeats you in one night even without a battle and makes you cower in fear," proclaimed Zeus from the heavens. "You will leave this plain of existence and join Ra forever to fight the serpent in the heavens."

Set, disappeared for ever without even a whimper.

Persæus shed his fur and covered his nakedness while his men looked on still horrified. He was indeed a great demi-god and they were all shaking with the adrenaline of fear. He walked over to them and they backed away just a step; he laughed. "Tomorrow you will be asking yourselves if this was just a dream."

"No," one of them said, "no, I don't think so."

Persæus and Achilles both laughed at the group of men. "I'm sure you will remember nothing," said Zeus and suddenly it was over; in their minds Persæus had simply stood his ground with Set and Set backed down. It wasn't quite a lie as in essence, that was what had happened. Achilles broke out a bottle of liquor and they all toasted to the success of the mission. It had ended far more easily than any had expected and even Zeus mentioned to Achilles, Danaë and Persæus privately in their minds, "I never knew Set to be such a coward. So disappointing, I was hoping for more of a show." And they laughed at the private joke.

They didn't stay much longer but Niccoli offered to secure the doors from the inside so the rest could go home and for which they were all grateful. He was a good man in every respect and he was loved by many around the small town for all he did to help his men. They all had memories of his generosity and his good will in hard times and this did not seem out of place for him. When they returned in the morning, they found him cold and lifeless. It appeared that his passing was peaceful. It was his time to go, it seemed he knew this and he would be missed terribly by all that knew him. It seemed he might have stayed at the shop on purpose so that they would find his body as he lived alone. They took the day off in his honor and to make arrangements for his interment. He had brought a lot to the company and the company made all the arrangements for a beautiful headstone and a place of honor in the cemetery where only the most famous and richest were buried. He would be remembered by half the town at his memorial service, there wasn't a dry eye in the place and the grass at his graveside was aptly watered by the tears of his mourners.

Achilles expressed to Persæus and Danaë his concerns that there might be others just as powerful in some fashion as had been Set and that they might also be looking to infiltrate The Works in some manner. The two agreed that he had a valid point and that they should somehow brace for more trouble. Achilles called his buyers and suppliers for word of any rumors of which he should be aware to no avail. If they knew of anything, they were not talking and that bothered him. There should be some type of murmur among the others in the trades yet they swore there was none. And so it was that Achilles, Persæus and Joseph began staying nights at the shop. Each would alternate an hour after work to go home and shower and change and Danaë made sure they ate well but it was still not the most relaxing way to live. It was a labor of love and commitment they were willing to make for the sake of the company they were building and very possibly for its very existence. Somehow the blessings of Zeus on the business were being misconstrued as a deadly competition.

It was only a matter of time before their caution was proven correct and there were multiple break in attempts. So far, only through the front doors; which were driven off simply by lighting the place up so that the apparent thieves realized there were people inside. These were likely petty criminals of a local variety as true professionals would come prepared for any occurrence and try to make something of the attempts. They were at a loss to figure out why; except that somehow the information about the vault had been blown out of proportion making it seem they might have some bounty that would make such an effort worthwhile. Had they only known why it had been built in the first place... But the men kept vigil regardless of the caliber of the criminals making these attempts knowing that sooner or later they would realize it was in vain; or the real thing would come along. It was only a matter of time before Ba'al arrived on their doorstep looking for his cousin, Set.

"You are looking in the wrong place for your cousin," decried Achilles when Ba'al came storming in on a cloudy morning.
"What have you done with my kin!" he demanded.
"We have done nothing with him, but have you checked with Ra?"
"He would not go there to that barge willingly! He was here to roust you who have taken over the metals trades by force and return the work to Egypt."
"Oh, you are mistaken; we have not taken the metals trades, they were given to us by Zeus, himself. And as for your cousin, he coward on our floor before running away like a child to take

refuge with Ra upon his boat in the heavens."

"You lie! Set is fearless! What have you done with him?"

Persæus wanted badly to transform to defend against this trash of a god that disturbed their lives with his menial attempt at intimidation; but Achilles cautioned him to wait with a wave of his hand. "Why have you really come here? What purpose can you hope to serve that Set did not accomplish you weakling?"

With that Ba'al was rightfully incensed and the wind blew and the rains came down and the men closed the doors of the shop to protect their work.

But Ba'al being especially angry brought the weather inside at which point Achilles gave Persæus the nod to deal with this minor player of the cosmos. It took only seconds for him to rise up in his full glory, wings spread and eyes bright red, changing the hue of everything around to that of a hellish landscape. A roar from deep within his giant persona shaking the very foundations of the warehouse and sending Ba'al to his knees, Persæus grabbed him up in one clawed hand and brought him up to eye level. Ba'al soiled himself and knew they had told the truth of cowardly Set. Persæus brought him up close to his nose sniffing and howled, "You pissed in my hand, you coward!"

Persæus flung him across the room where he hit the wall leaving an impression. Persæus shook the urine and feces from his hand in disgust. The men not remembering the last transformation thanks to Zeus, hid behind machinery shaking in fear. Who wouldn't? Ba'al recovered himself and begged for mercy from Persæus, "Please, oh winged demon, spare me. I did not mean to offend."

"You lie! Ba'al, the liar from Egypt, come here to intimidate and offend and then you lie! You soil yourself instead."

"I beg of thee, do not eat me!"

"Why would I eat some piss and feces covered imbecile that stinks. And you are ugly!" Persæus didn't know why he called him ugly, it just came to mind and seemed to be the right thing to do.

"Leave now, do not return and tell others of what you have seen here today! Tell them not to bother us anymore!"

The skies had begun to clear.

"Yes, great and powerful demon! What is your name that I may tell of your incredible mercy?"

"I am Persæus, the destroyer, the ravager of worlds and consumer of the wicked."

"Yes, great and mighty Persæus the destroyer!"

"Yes, the ravager and consumer of the wicked! Remember that part also. Memorize it!"

Achilles had started laughing as he appreciated Persæus' humor.

"Hey, Achilles! Come on dude, I'm trying to make an impression here."

"Oh, I'm sure by the wet spot in his robes that you have made an adequate impression."

At this point Achilles could hardly contain himself and even Persæus laughed. A deep, growling, rather disturbing laugh. In fact, Achilles commented to that affect.

"That's disturbing."

"Vile interloper, Ba'al. Leave here now and tell all that you meet that I am here to greet them and I will eat whomever dares to come in."

"Yes, great Persæus the destroyer, ravager of worlds and consumer of the wicked!"

"Okay, that's more like it."

Persæus shrank down to his seven-foot self, folded his wings and walked over to Ba'al, "So, we understand each other?"

"Yes, Persæus!"

"That's Persæus the destroyer, the ravager of worlds and consumer of the wicked."

"Yes, Persæus the destroyer, the ravager of worlds and consumer of the wicked."

Persæus looked at Achilles and asked, "What do they teach these gods in schools today?"

Achilles was just about rolling on the floor and the men of the shop had come out from behind their hiding spots to enjoy the show; although none got very close.

"Fine, leave our presence."

With that Ba'al ran out the man door in the front and they never heard from him again.

Achilles called out, "Zeus! We need that memory thing you do!"

Zeus replied, "Can't you at least show a bit of respect when you call on me?"

"Oh, great and powerful Zeus, father of all, please do your memory trick?"

"Oh, fine. Persæus, you might want to put on some street clothes?"

Persæus made a hasty exit to the office where he kept an extra change of clothes and Zeus did his thing, "All right, everyone, but Ba'al is taken care of. No one will believe him anyway, The great liar and deceiver, Ba'al."

"Thank you, great and powerful, Zeus!"

"Oh, stop it, now you're just being ridiculous."

"Yes, sir" Achilles said contritely.

At that moment Persæus came out of the office and said, "Thank you father. Did you enjoy the show?"

"Yes son, that was the first time I've ever seen Ba'al soil himself. You made quite the impression on him."

And with that, Zeus was gone. Persæus proceeded to clean up his fur from the floor.

"That's what I love about father's visits. Always congenial but short and sweet."

The thunder rolled in the distance and the two men looked at each other and laughed. They loved their relationship with the high god of Olympus and couldn't imagine a life otherwise. They were happy to have his favor.

When the day's work was finished, they decided to have a short meeting with the men and Achilles asked, "Did you all enjoy meeting Ba'al?"

The men looked at each other and had no clue about what he was speaking and with that he dismissed it by saying, "I guess he was in and out to fast. I'm sorry you missed him. We are not going to replace Niccoli just yet, he would be hard to replace and I want to be careful about whom we choose for such a position. It won't hurt us to honor his memory a bit longer."

To which the men murmured their approval; their love for his memory being very strong.

I'm having an alarm system installed tomorrow so if any of you come in on the weekend to do any little projects, be sure that Persæus, Joseph or myself is here to disarm it. We will be the only ones with the code. You know we are usually around anyway so it shouldn't create any problems. I have found someone to help Danaë with the office load. She has been gracious in helping us so far but she needs help with business doing as well as it is. She will switch to part time when our new office manager gets up to speed. Isis will be starting her training tomorrow and I want you all to be on your best behavior. I've hired her against my better judgement, because of her qualifications being stellar; but she's also quite the beauty and I want you all to be aware that I will tolerate no fraternization. Not because I'm against it but because her brother is Set." Everyone commented among themselves on that bit of news. "I don't want any more trouble from that guy. It shouldn't be an issue as long as we all behave… Persæus."

Everyone laughed as he turned red at the implication.

"Okay, that's all I needed, Persæus, Joseph, anything you guys need to say? No? Okay, have a good night, gentlemen."

Persæus pulled Achilles aside and asked, "The sister of Set? Really? Is that wise?"

"She claims she doesn't like her brother and with him on Ra's barge? It's worth taking a chance and she is highly qualified. We need to keep someone in here that can keep us running on an even keel."

"Okay, I'm willing if you think it's safe. I hope you're right."

With that, they closed down the warehouses and they all went home for the first time in weeks.

In the morning, they found the shop had remained intact

overnight as they'd hoped and the weather was shaping up to be pleasant from what they could tell. Things were moving along quite nicely until Isis walked in. It was as though the entire shop saw her at once and everyone just stopped to stare. She was certainly every bit as beautiful as Achilles had said and they could not help but look upon her with the greatest admiration. Tall for most women, especially in her three-inch heels, her limbs long and lean, hair in a golden barrette at the back of her head, hanging below her waist with the skin of a Persian goddess. Breasts like pomegranates her beauty could easily rival that of Nefertari. Looking crisp in a white long-sleeved silk blouse with pearls around her neck and a black skirt that covered her knees she was the image of a proper queen and the pride of some father's soul. Achilles was right, Isis was a couple of years older than Persæus but he was smitten and Danaë had her eye on him. Persæus had not escaped Isis' notice either and the interactions in the first five minutes were so obvious that they were comical. Achilles hoped he'd made a good decision.

Danaë would keep Isis busy for now and Achilles would try and keep Pereus at heel and on a leash if he could. But the hormones were obviously going to take their course, hopefully at a slow and predictable pace. Danaë put Isis right to work showing her the filing requirements along with order and supply procurement and fulfillment along with the hot file system for orders in process. Thank Zeus they kept the hot files on the outside of the office so the men did not have to go inside except on rare occasion.

Danaë realized that Isis would be plenty busy to start with and that she was likely to keep her nose clean for a bit but She wasn't so sure about Persæus. The ring Isis wore on her ring finger was a deterrent of course but it didn't take long for Danaë to figure out that it was just there to ward off the evil spirits of the male persuasion. Still, that bode well for Isis and it gave Danaë some hope of not becoming a grandmother too soon. Danaë would continue to pass out the paychecks to the men for now and that would stave things off a bit longer. She knew how to run interference and she had promised Achilles she'd do her best; unbeknownst to any of the men or Persæus.

Achilles had split most of Niccoli's responsibilities between Persæus and Joseph as opposed to taking them on himself and he decided he needed to put the younger men to work on some of the outside sales as well. That would keep them busier for the time being. Yes, this was going to prove to be a bit of a challenge but it might just work out. Achilles had to admit, it was nice to have two pieces of eye candy working in the office these days.
"I heard that!" came the voice of Zeus in his head.
"You know I would never approach her. That doesn't change the fact that she is nice to look at."
"Just remember, look and don't touch. She is your auntie, after all. Not that it would stop some of the gods."
"Yes, sire. I keep reminding myself. I know also, that she is completely faithful to you."
Zeus laughed, he knew how Achilles must feel and he was actually sympathetic. After all, she had held his own attention for nearly twenty years.

Having deterred Ba'al as well as Set was a great victory for them all but Achilles had to know, "Zeus, will Horace be a problem?"
"I can't say for sure, but he has not been a fan of Set or Ba'al since Set plucked out his eyes. He's less bitter since he got them back but I don't think he will help in any way."
"That's good to know, thank you."
"Don't get to all sure and cocky about it, things change and I don't get out to Egypt much, I only suspect things are about the same."
"That's fair enough. Thank you for the blessings of work for all of us by the way. I don't know if I've said that enough."
"No, you haven't, but I see it in your heart and I know you appreciate it. It is just that you be rewarded for caring after

Persæus and watching after Danaë."

"Yes, it is and it allows me to take care of my men also."

"You're getting as arrogant as me!"

"You are a good example."

"If you were not one of my favorites…"

"I know that also."

"Goodbye, little god."

Achilles laughed as Zeus made his departure. He was thinking he might have to lighten up on the old man but then again, no. Times had changed and so had Zeus, he was so much better to get along with and he gave them all hope and the grace to persevere unlike the eon's past. It was more like having a family instead of the old days when the gods fought among themselves and only tortured the humans they used and abused. Achilles was liking this knew Zeus and the world he was shaping; all since his son had come along, it was as though a whole new chapter had been opened.

It was funny how many of their customers had come by when Danaë had first started working in the office and it seemed now, that even more were stopping in to make their orders in person since Isis had begun working with them. Achilles couldn't find fault with their curiosity and he certainly wasn't going to complain about orders being up by ten percent. That more than paid for Isis' salary and now that Niccoli had passed that was a salary he was not paying. It was a really terrible way to look at the savings but facts were facts and every little bit helped the bottom line; and the shelves in the vault were filling ever faster. Achilles had to hire his engineer friend once again. This time not to construct a vault but to help streamline the flow of work through the shops. They had tried to create a situation where the work came in one side and left at the other but they were still tripping over one another at times and Achilles felt there must be something more they could do.

Indeed, there was, according to the engineer and he would be happy to help out for a price. If he could help keep them from needing to buy another warehouse for a while, it would be worth it. Joseph worked with the engineer to lay out the proposed changes while Persæus kept the flow going in both warehouses. Before long holes were made at the forward end of both buildings and a second passage was created. The materials deliveries no longer had to be carted to the rear of the second building but were dropped at the front where it was a straight shot across the new passage into the first building. Both buildings had their own circuitous routes for the work flow that rotated counter clockwise and the finished products ended up at the front doors again for delivery. It was a minor stroke of genius and it worked slick to make things move faster while leaving the centers of each building open for the fabrication of even larger structures. The small parts building started to take on some of the smaller large parts and the large parts became larger. It was music to the eyes.

When the building to the other side of the original warehouse came up for sale, Achilles bought it even though he didn't need it quite yet. It was convenient to have it available for the future and for now, he would move the shipping and the receiving departments into there in their entirety. It made sense to have shipping and receiving all in the same area as it required only one loading dock and with a passage directly through the front of all three buildings it was a breeze to move parts and materials. Achilles assigned the new department to Danaë to get it organized and started and then had her cross train, Isis. Eventually Isis moved over to the third building and she was no longer in view of the men, specifically Persæus; and Danaë moved back over to scheduling. That also relieved Danaë of a great deal of the paperwork shuffle and now Isis could be in charge of Shipping and receiving and hire on the people she felt she needed. They were growing so quickly they were the premier employer in town. It created some extreme jealousy for a few but mostly people respected and congratulated them on their success.

Zeus dropped in in person one evening while the executive crew were partaking of some libations. Joseph and Leon had never met Zeus in person and although Isis was familiar with him, she was not a fan, but she respected him. She was apparently not aware that Zeus was Persæus father. Achilles was just announcing that Joseph would take over as President of the small parts production operation and that Leon would be the Vice President. Joseph and Leon immediately bowed the knee and since they were not gods or demi-gods Zeus did not give them leeway.

"Rise humans," was all he said.

"Well, it seems you are doing well enough that I might ask a favor of you, Achilles."

"Of, course. If it is within my power to give to you, Zeus; I owe you everything, including my life!"

"Well, yes, yes you do," Zeus was rubbing it in and Danaë smiled at Achilles obvious discomfort. After all the familiarity Zeus had allowed Achilles, he was enjoying making him squirm just a bit. "There is a man in Athens that has been very faithful in honoring me and he has fallen on hard times. You know I don't generally help just any human, there are just too many of them and they breed like rats." Joseph and Leon were a bit taken a back. "You boys don't get your panties in a bunch, if you could see things from where I sit, you'd understand. In this one case, Alex has been particularly useful to me and he has taken on a lot responsibility in his community. I was hoping you would take a look at his operation and see if you could make his business a subsidiary of yours?"

"If it's possible, consider it done, father," said Persæus.

The look of shock on Isis' face was startling and all in the room knew this was a revelation for her. How she didn't know was almost beyond comprehension. Danaë put a comforting hand no top of the hand of Isis.

"What are you drinking this evening?" inquired Zeus.

"This drink is from the Northern regions; they call it vodka. Not much flavor, but it will grow hair on your chest."

"Then why are you letting the ladies drink it? Here let me try it." That lightened the mood a bit and even Isis' stoney face broke into a smile. She had not realized that Zeus could have a sense of humor, she had only heard negative things of him in Egypt.

"Yes, Isis. I was once a very stern god but life changes and so did I. Oh, you didn't realize I am omniscient? Yes, it kind of goes with the whole god thing, at least it does on Olympus. This vodka stuff isn't all that great. I'll stick to that almond drink you had a bit ago."

"Here, let me get you some. Where do we find, Alex, father?"

"He is in an area called Water Square. When you get there, just call for me and I will walk with you. It has been far too long since I have walked among my people. Yes, I like this almond drink; very nice, thank you."

And he was gone again.

"So, just like that?" queried Isis.

"Just like that," said the three that knew him well; and they laughed.

Achilles and Persæus traveled by train to Athens the next day. And found their way to Water Square. At least it was near a place where Alex could ship his goods easily. They called to Zeus and he appeared in his street clothes that he had taken to wearing but this time his olive leaf crown was not present.

"Probably good that you came incognito."

"You just love playing with fire, don't you, Achilles?"

Smiling he responded, "Well, you seem to take it well these days and we do laugh when we are together."

"Good thing for you."

"Now father…"

They chatted as they walked and a few times people jumped up as they passed by shouting, "I'm healed!"

"I miss times like this, I need to do it more often," said Zeus.

They finally came to a small shop that looked run down but it had three men working hard inside with little ventilation on what appeared to be widgets of a nature neither Achilles nor Persæus had seen before.

"We are here to speak with Alex, if he is available."

A fourth man came from the back of the small shop, "I'm Alex, how may I help you fine gentlemen?"

"We had heard you have a small business here and we wanted to see what your shop can handle. We may have some business we can give to you to manufacture in our stead."

"I'm not looking a gift horse in the mouth, but may I inquire as to how you heard of us?"

"We have a common friend that said you could use the work and we have several customers in this area. It would be very helpful if you could fulfill those orders for us," said Achilles.

"Who are you gentlemen?"

"I am Achilles and this is my cousin Persæus, I own A & N The Works."

All four men dropped their tools and greeted them enthusiastically. "We know of your business and we are glad to help you in any way we can!" exclaimed Alex.

Achilles continued, "We would like to make your company a subsidiary of A & N The Works. That means we would buy your company. You are still in control and you guide it even though you would be selling it to us. We will keep you in charge, it will all be in writing. That way we have a presence here, you make the parts for the companies that are in this area and our shipping costs go down. Everyone wins and you get to increase your business and maybe get raises in your salaries. Does this sound interesting to you?"

"So, it would no longer belong to me?"

"Technically, no. But we can stipulate in the contract that you make all the decisions as long as we feel it benefits your business. I know that sounds like you lose control but you won't. We don't have the time to micromanage what you do here so you will have a board of directors, possibly the men you have here?"

Thats the four of you running it almost like being partners. Would you like to think about it?"

"Well, could we have a week?"

"I'm afraid that won't be possible," said Zeus.

He had not revealed himself to this point, but Alex knew well who's voice he was hearing and he dropped to one knee.

"My Lord! I did not recognize you!"

"I expect not. I have heard your prayers and supplications and I have asked these two to step in to help. You have been a good and faithful servant. Achilles and Persæus love me also and they will do whatever is needed to help your business. I recommend you sell to them and I guarantee they will make your lives better."

"Of course, Lord. On your word and without hesitation."

"Very good. Achilles, give him the papers to have his attorney look at them."

"Why did I come along, father?"

"You're the muscle in case they gave us any trouble."

The four old gentlemen looked at Zeus and then at Persæus, "This is your father?" asked Alex in dismay.

"I got lucky and look more like my mother," teased Persæus.

Zeus shook his head and asked in exasperation, "Why do I put up with the two of you?"

Achilles said, "Because we are the comedic relief."

The gentlemen looked at the three and then at each other not believing the conversation.

"We've known each other a while," said Zeus.

Alex responded, "May we live long enough to know you that well."

Zeus smiled and said, "I doubt it, but I'll see what I can do."

The gentlemen laughed hesitantly but thought that was very kind of Zeus.

Zeus continued, "Boys, what do you say we go to lunch and let Alex run that to his attorney. I haven't had any actual food in a while. Maybe they serve that Almond liquor here somewhere."

"Just down the street at Gyros' Pub," said Alex.

"Outstanding!" exclaimed Zeus. "Will two hours be enough?"

"If he is there and not in court, my Lord."

"All right then. I'll make sure that happens," Zeus winked at Alex as being omniscient, he already knew the outcome. "Boys, let's go see if we can develop a drinking problem; I'm pretty good at this comedy stuff too. Giraffe? Platypus? You haven't seen anything yet."

It was so far out of character for Zeus to spend this much time with them the two men almost felt uncomfortable and Achilles asked what was up.

"What? I can't spend time with my son and his cousin?"

"But you never have," said Achilles. "Not that I'm complaining, this has been truly amazing and to see you care for Alex and his men is truly an eye opener. I never thought you to be that compassionate toward mortals."

"Achilles, Persæus, I know at times it must seem that I don't care or that I don't want to be around but that's just not so. I simply can't. This is not my only concern, nor is it the only world on which I have children. I let my children take care of themselves so they might grow to be better beings and those that choose to go awry usually end up destroying themselves. I can live with that. I have to live with that, it is the natural way of things; it's how the universe was created. But when my children pray in earnest, I listen and often I'm able to give a nudge here and there that is of benefit to more than just the few that actually want my help. Those are the times to which I give the most priority because it helps the most while those that ask, learn the lessons they must. Those around them and are most affected by them learn also and the world grows in the right direction."

"So, war and pestilence?" asked Persæus.

"Those are mostly of man's making when they have allowed themselves to be influenced by the likes of Ba'al and Set and any number of other unsavory types that exist. So many blame the gods when in fact they should only blame their brothers and sisters for allowing the influence of vile and unrighteous desires."

"But Ba'al and Set are gods, aren't they?"

"Yes, in their own right, but they are not allowed on Olympus except by special invitation. There will come a time when they will be relegated to the underworld, to Hades and Anubis; I will put them as far as the East is from the West and they will be heard of no more."

"When will that time come, father?"

"In terms of eternity, it is almost upon us but in mortal terms, it will happen when it happens."

"It all sounds rather liquid," said Persæus.

"Now you're beginning to understand. I knew this time with you would be fruitful. Let's go back to Alex' shop and see if we can find a larger space for them. Under your company's influence, they will need it very soon."

"You already know what it is we will find, don't you?"

"Being omniscient does have its advantages."

The men walked past Alex' place as he was not yet back and the three men that worked for him were eating lunches they had brought from home. They waved as they passed by to be congenial and down the road a piece, in about a block they came across an abandoned warehouse that was sorely in need of roof repair and some window replacement.

"What do you think, boys," asked Zeus. "Do you think this would work?"

"Well, I don't see why not," Replied Achilles. "It needs more repair than I'd like to invest but I suppose if we can get it at the right price."

"I suspect that could be arranged," said Zeus.

"Oh, do you?" asked Persæus.

Achilles remarked, "I think I like this advantage. Would you care to tell us the outcome?"

"Well, I have to leave some things to the imagination."

"Alrighty then! Do you want to tell us who to contact to purchase the property?"

"Let's let Alex sign the papers first and then ask him, shall we?"

The men walked back to Alex' place to find him just arriving back from his attorney's office. He acted quite glad to see them just now arriving back also and immediately noted, "My attorney pointed out only a couple of things to clarify."

"Okay, go," said Achilles.

"First and foremost, you have left blank the price. I don't expect much but I do want to take care of my men so I need 100,000 Euros for the business. It is a good location and we have established customers so this is three times our annual gross which is fairly standard for a business."

"Done," Replied Achilles.

That was not expected at all as the business wasn't worth even close to that much but to obtain the customer base, the reputation and the good will of the men involved, it was necessary and Achilles recognized this. He wasn't going to crush them to get what Zeus wanted.

"Next," Alex stammered, as Achilles' acceptance of the price threw him off base, "You have specified that we keep only fifty percent of the profits and we will need sixty."

"We need to recoup our investment as quickly as possible so we must get fifty percent. But we can work with you on that. Fifty percent this year, you get fifty-five next year and sixty the year after. That's more than anyone else will pay."

"You're making this too easy, what's your game?"

"No game, we want everyone to win, is that so wrong?"

"Wrong, no. Extremely unusual? Pretty much," said Alex.

"Okay, we are strange. Now that we have established that, can we get down to signing?"

Alex looked at his men questioningly like he couldn't believe this was happening. They all looked back at him and just shrugged their shoulders as they knew it was ultimately up to him.

He put the papers on the table, filled in the blanks and signed. It was done, they were a subsidiary of A & N The Shop.

Zeus took Alex by the arm and said, "Would you mind walking down the street to your new location? I'm assuming you know who we need to speak to in order to purchase this warehouse?"

"Me…"

"I thought so."

Achilles and Persæus just started laughing. It now made sense that Zeus had this made in Olympus deal ready for them to purchase and he knew exactly what to expect. That omniscient thing was definitely a step up in business.

"Okay, Alex," said Achilles, "We've been good to you in every respect. What is your rock-bottom price on the warehouse, this travesty that needs to be rebuilt from the ground up?"

"You want to buy this and move us in here?"

"That's the plan, you'll need the space in short order."

"Well, I bought it twenty years ago for €50,000. I own it outright. The taxes have cost me €80,000 over twenty years. It's now valued at €120,000. How about €200,000?"

"I can't do that, Alex. If I do, you know the city and state will tax it at the €200,000 level. If you can sell for €130,000 due to the massive amount of work it needs, can we do that?"

"€150,000?"

"€140,000."

"Well, I guess I could argue but you're pulling our fat from the fire already. It's a deal."

"Thank you for working with us on that. I will have your money transferred in the morning. Would you care to see to the rebuild on the place? Getting the bids, hiring the contractors and such?"

"Of course! It's to everyone's advantage."

"All right. I'm going to have the contracts and blueprints on the parts you'll be producing for us, delivered over the next couple of days and you get on the horn with me to ensure we get production started as quickly as possible. You'll also be speaking to Danaë in scheduling and Isis in shipping and receiving for the next few months. Write those names down. Persæus and Joseph are the VPs in charge of large and small parts production, respectively, and you'll need to speak with them from time to time. I'll send you a company breakdown and phone list so you know who everyone is. I'll bet you didn't see your day going like this when you got up this morning?"

"No, sir!"

"Welcome to The Works family. You're going to love working with us."

"I certainly hope so, sir."

"Don't worry, Alex," said Zeus. "This is the best day of your life and the lives of your men, I guarantee it!"

"Yes, Lord. If you say so, Lord."

"I do."

And with that, Zeus was gone and the men along with Alex stared where he had stood.

"Don't worry, one gets used to it," said Achilles.

"Sort of," said Persæus, "we need to get back to our own men and production and we have disturbed you long enough for one day."

"Thank you, so much, you have given us hope for all the labors we have expended."

"I'm glad Zeus asked us to come and meet with you," said Achilles, we will speak further tomorrow when I have everything ready to go."

With that the two men shook hands with Alex and his men and left for the train back North and to their own business and family. It was a bit of a walk back to the train but it was a happy one and they felt they had fulfilled a great need not only for the men of Alex and himself but also for their own customers and business. As Achilles had said to Alex previously, it was a win/win for them all. He felt it was a good fit and Persæus agreed. They could reduce shipping costs considerably and it would make delivery times shorter for this area where they had several customers.

Persæus had done the calculations in his head and he suspected that the percentages that Alex had agreed to would hurt them a bit on the return on investment but if they increased sales in the area just a bit more, they could make up for it within two to three years. The purchase would pay for itself and they'd be running in the black because they had not taken a bank loan. Buying in for cash was the key to making the deal work. So often businesses tried to expand through bank loans which, in and of itself was not a bad thing, but it simply cost a lot more than paying cash. They didn't mind using their own cash regardless of what the so-called experts said. If the deal wasn't good enough to risk one's own money, the deal simply wasn't good enough.

The evening was cooling off nicely and the boys were happy to make the train just before it pulled out of the station. It lessened the time sitting and feeling like they were unproductive. Something they both had come to appreciate for themselves and for their men. The conversation waned and they both fell asleep after the relative excitement of the day. Neither of them had any expectation of the business growing in such a manner and it was a bit overwhelming. One always hopes they have a winning business model and often even that is not enough to create success. But having Zeus on their side was far more than most could hope and he had certainly kept his promise to Achilles to bless his business for the expenditure of building the vault to maintain Achilles during his time of trial and temptation.

They arrived back home and stopped off at the shop to double check everything as that was just a habit they'd developed over the years they had been together. It was wisdom in case there was a need and it simply helped them sleep at night. They knew they could trust Joseph and Leon or they would not hold the positions of importance that they did; but it never hurt to verify that trust they had developed. There were a few minutes left in the day so Achilles called Danaë and Isis into a small setting with Leon, Joseph and Persæus to recap the successful business of the day. He also wanted to give them a heads up of the expectations of the morning in getting Alex and his men up to speed. It was also a warning that they could be spending a good deal of time on the phone explaining, perhaps more than once, how things were to be done.

He did not expect the new location to be efficient any time terribly soon but he wanted to be sure everyone here did their best to make the startup and transition as smooth as possible. The men at the new location were older, after all, and maybe not quite as energetic or up on modern business practices as Achilles would have hoped, but he knew that Zeus would not have steered him wrong bringing them on board. He warned everyone to be patient with the new location. Everyone at business location one (BLO), as they would now call it, was very excited and couldn't wait to get things transferred over to business location two (BLT). They suddenly felt like they were part of the big time and big business; and the three-letter reference made them all hungry. They actually knew they were still puny but that they were well on their way. It was an exciting time and the news was quite welcome and celebrated.

The bunch of alcoholics they were becoming, they celebrated with Zeus favorite almond liquor and although they invited him, he didn't respond; the busy life of a god. He had, after all, spent a great deal of the day with the boys for the first time that any of them could recall. They each took their own moment to thank him for that as it was truly out of character and truly appreciated; even Isis, who was now understanding better who he really was. It was a red-letter day and they marked it on the company calendar to remember in the future as a day of growth and a day of fondness toward Zeus. He was making them all believers in his benevolence that none of them had actually seen or understood in the past. He was not so much like his son Ares of Hera, often called Mars, the god of war, but more like a true father to all his children. Today he had made himself loveable to all under Achilles' watchful eye and that made Danaë much more confident for their next child residing within her womb.

CHAPTER SIX:
GROWTH IN SO MANY
NEW RESPECTS

Persæus knew immediately that Danaë was pregnant with his sister. It was only new knowledge to her but he sensed it from his conquered demons that now lived and loved within him. The time he'd spent with the entities within, he had tamed them and taught them of love and submission which the Nephilim especially rebelled but finally accepted. They would conquer him if they could and go about their devious ways, but they knew that it was not possible and they submitted willingly to avoid the battle they knew they couldn't win and that might also kill them. Persæus was at peace with his demons and he enjoyed their company at times, visiting and teaching them of things greater than the vile pursuits to which they were prone. That didn't stop them from trying to tempt him on occasion, but it had become more comic relief for him as they just had no clue of that which they were up against. Ya, he was that good. And as powerful as they both were, they were monsters after all and not capable of defeating someone of faith and love.

When he had first conquered them, they disappeared from his knowledge but as time had proceeded, he noticed their footprints I many of his thoughts. They were still present; they were just wise enough to stay out of the way. He invited them to sit around the campfire of his mind at night such that he could get to know their strengths, evils and weaknesses. To know their full power, he had to know them well without allowing them access to his control over them. He spent the time to get to know them and learn of their exceptional strengths, far beyond what he had ever expected and felt that they were friends, although not quite ones to be trusted. It was a relationship that he did not confide in his mother or Achilles as he feared their concept of the situation. But Zeus knew and in fact, had warned him of the pitfalls possible and kept Persæus safe; much to his demons' chagrin. It was not a relationship he necessarily enjoyed but one of necessity for his use of his own full strength, should it ever be needed. You may have heard people say, "I do what the voices in my head tell me." It's funny but in the case of Persæus it was true, to a degree; he listened but hardly ever did as they said. After all, they had not fully embraced the goodness that he implored upon them.

Times were good and the new shop in Athens developed well and prospered strengthening their place in the local market and breaking into the worldwide market. They were even selling to companies in Cairo, Egypt which likely upset Ba'al and Set, but after the garbage those two tried to pull they could only congratulate themselves. Set had finally come off of Ra's barge as his courage returned but he hadn't shown his face in Phthia since then. Life was good and they were loving it. Hunting season was upon them again and they had not gone the last year; things had been too crazy at the time and they simply had to skip it. This year they had promised themselves they would make it, by hook or by crook, as the saying went. They were hoping they could get their normal sight on the pond again this year but there was no telling until they got there. Working ahead on the schedule they were able get some time set up to close the shop and allow everyone to go at the same time. You'd think they spent enough time together at work but it just wasn't the same as the bonding they experienced in the woods around a camp fire.

They were able to plan the trip over a month end weekend with a Friday in one month and a Monday in the next. That way it not only eased scheduling requirements but also split the time off between two pay periods. The company had grown considerably and they had to rent another truck to carry men and equipment this time. Isis and Danaë not being hunters themselves, each took a day to answer phones while the men were all gone and therefore each got an extra day off as well. Friday morning early, they set out for the pond with eighteen of the forty men from work in the hunting party. It promised to be a good time and the reports they'd heard described large herds and plentiful large bucks. Several of the men had purchased blinds for the hunt this year and Persæus thought he might try joining them in one if there was room. He had always just sat in the brush to hide from the game but he could understand the usefulness of such a thing, especially with so many of them in the same area.

They were able to get their favorite area as they'd hoped and had lunch before the evening hunt started. The woods seemed empty of other hunters this year in spite of the reports of good herds. But that just meant it would be safer and hopefully more productive for their party. Even the herd trails appeared to be larger and more well-worn this year, that was always a good sign. It was hard to say why, possibly because of the size of the party but not a single animal was sighted that evening, although there was plenty of sign confirming the stories of plentiful animals. Persæus opted to sit above the feed waters of the pond on a trail he'd spotted up there for a couple of hours that evening just after dark hoping to see something. The Red Fallow herd came trotting down the trail with the buck in the lead, his rack just barely fitting between the undergrowth on both sides, the dos following casually behind with their fawns now showing spikes so they were legal to take. There were easily thirty animals and they all appeared healthy, none were lame or limping and they appeared well fed.

They stopped at the feeder stream that led to the pond and they drank heavily while the buck and a do kept watch and when he lowered his head to drink, three of the females were watching. Persæus didn't dare move a muscle or even breath heavily as they were so near to him. He could smell them and that indicated that he was down wind of the herd and they couldn't smell him. He watched until they started to leave and noticed they were not heading to the fork in the trail that led to the pond. It seemed odd and after they had proceeded, he walked down the other trail to see if there was a discernable reason they avoided that direction. Persæus smelled the reason before he found it. Not far down the trail he found the remains of another hunter that were well decomposed. He could tell it was a hunter by the bow lying next to him still gripped by the rotting hand and the camouflage clothing that remained somewhat intact. The three arrows in his back indicated his obvious demise by murder and Persæus could only guess that his hunting partner was to blame. He didn't touch the body as he didn't want to disturb any evidence and realized that someone would need to return to civilization, or at least to find cell service and call it in. The pond area would be useless for hunting with all the law enforcement that would be called in to investigate. He went back to the camp and informed the party they needed to reevaluate the area of their hunt.

Achilles sent one of the drivers out to find cell service and alert the local police while Persæus described his findings and suggested that the morning hunt proceed above the pond and set up their blinds along the game trial up there. The driver was back within the hour and led the police to the camp where Persæus spoke with them of his discovery. He led them to the body which thankfully didn't smell quite as bad in the cool of the night and they cordoned off the area. They questioned everyone in the hunting party as though they might be involved which made everyone very uncomfortable and even angry as they only just arrived in the area. But that's how police tend to be, they call it being thorough when in many if not most cases they are looking for the easiest person to hang. They spent an especially long-time questioning Persæus as he had discovered the body. They checked all of his equipment trying to match his arrows to the ones in the body. But by Midnight they finally realized their investigation was clearing everyone at the camp. But they managed to set a very dark tone for the night and a very tired camp come morning.

The hunters realized the authorities would be back at first light and they determined to be up and sitting in their blinds before that. Achilles was up first and had coffee perking and bacon cooking before four a.m. Joseph warmed some bread and made sure the butter was softened near the fire. The others started stirring when the odiferous meal was nearly ready and they all commiserated over the short night of sleep. It didn't take long for them all to have a bite and a drink and they were heading up stream with their equipment looking for spots with a clear view of the trail but far enough back to keep the Deer from noticing their scent. There was no breeze at all that morning so that would help them stay hidden. It wasn't long before the sun started to brighten the sky and the stars disappeared. And it wasn't long after that the very same herd Persæus had seen the night before started wandering up the game trail. Again, the animals stopped to drink at the stream and as they did, most of the party loosed their arrows into a great deal of the animals The buck of course realized it was his time to die if he didn't move out and he was gone in an instant, but most of the others fell victim to men that were hungry to restock their freezers with venison.

They drug their kills away from the game trial and began to bleed and gut them just as the authorities could be heard arriving. They had no clue how rude they were being, talking and calling to each other there in the hunting area. Some of the men lamented they should just hang some human meat in the limbs for cutting up and salting. They would never do such a thing but that's what a nuisance the investigators were being. A few of the men had thought to bring shovels so they could bury the guts and not destroy the trail with the scent of death and they made short work of the whole situation. The larger animals were quartered and the smaller ones left whole to carry back to the camp and it took only a half hour to make the three trips necessary to get all the meat back to camp. Several men made themselves useful by getting out he ropes and raising the carcasses into the limbs while others cut some up and salted it and hung it over the fire for eating later. They would bring one of the quarters down later to cut up some steaks as well.

They enjoyed the fact that the police had not destroyed the hunt completely by their obnoxious appearance so early and noisy that morning. But then a couple of the officers decided to be especially rude and came in to camp asking to see the hunter's papers allowing them to hunt. With that Persæus and Achilles asked to see the commanding officer and there were words flying that neither of them usually used. With Persæus immense size and Achilles commanding and assertive presence from being a businessman for so many years it wasn't long before the officer in charge knew they had pushed too hard and that these were not men with which they could trifle. They backed down and left the camp before things escalated to a level they did not want to see. Several of the men that had gotten their kill for the hunt decided it was best to load up one of the trucks and head back to town, to get away from the corrupt authorities and back to their families. The rest, mostly the single guys decided to stay at least one more night to do the evening hunt and have some drinks around the camp fire.

Come midafternoon the police were still tramping about the woods and there would be no game in this particular area so the men sufficed to go looking for other viable areas to hunt come morning. It was reasonable to assume the animals might come back in a day after the police cleared out but not likely before that. They decided to follow the game trail away from the area and see where that led them and they did find a point where two trails crossed. That might be a premium location and they set up their blinds around the area for morning. Back at camp a quarter was lowered and steaks were cut for the evening meal. Achilles, as was tradition, got out a couple of bottles of wine and spirits and they enjoyed themselves as much as they could and did not ask the officers to join them. It ended up being a very good evening in spite of the situation and shortly after dark, the officers had completed their investigation, packed up and were gone. They didn't bother to say goodbye and that was probably a wise move after all of the feathers they had ruffled.

It was truly a good night with the men and they at one point broke into song which had never happened before. Must have been the alcohol… It made for some laughs because none of them were good singers. Come morning they were refreshed compared to the day before, they were up, coffeed, fed and nearly to their blinds when they spotted a brown bear. They stopped and watched as they couldn't bring it down, Brown bears, although stable in Greece were at threat of extinction and it was nearly a mortal sin to take on in a hunt or otherwise. They stayed mostly in the Rodopis Mountains and were very seldom seen this far south. With an estimated population of only 450 it was indeed odd to find one in this forest. They watched until it finally moved off and then headed for their blinds. The sun was already coming up by that time and they had not seen any animals yet, it was discouraging but they knew it was just a matter of time and patience before they might see a herd.

They sat at the intersection of trails until mid-morning without any action but they could see there was fresh spore on the trail which indicated they should eventually see something. Then as they were getting ready to go back to camp, they heard motion in the underbrush. The deer were not traveling the trial today, they were foraging alongside it. They must not have gotten their fill because the moon was not shining full at night this weekend. The deer were usually bedded down by this time of the morning. Soon the men could see their shapes among the bushes and they knew they could take at least a few of them. They shot almost simultaneously and there were five animals laying on the ground. That would fill out their limit for the number of men they had. It had been very successful in spite of things not going quite as planned. It seemed the reports of abundant game had been correct and they'd been able to take advantage of it. It was a good morning and the men got to dressing the animals and taking them back to camp. They would stay the night one more time and head back to town come morning. Most of them decided to take a morning nap as although they had caught up on some of their sleep, they wanted to enjoy the night around the campfire again.

It turned out that one of the men was a pretty good baker and had brought cinnamon pastries he broke out for them all to share. It was a nice surprise and it topped off nicely the lunch Persæus had cooked for them. Of course, they had more venison steaks but Persæus added some scrambled eggs with a light white flour gravy over it all and vegetables sautéed in butter combined with a light red wine vinaigrette. They were camping in style and panache! It helped make up for the police invasion of their camp and peace of mind. Come evening Achilles again provided the libations and since they weren't getting up early for the hunt a couple of them cut loose a bit and imbibed a bit heavily. No one cared as they were all generally happy drunks and mostly, no one caused any trouble. It was a good time together and they would be rested and back to their labors in only two more days anyway. Why not have fun?

As the evening progressed, they each fell asleep from all the activity of the weekend and now the effect of the alcohol and soon the fire burned down to the sound of snoring. The deep, alcohol assisted sleep could quite possibly have been blamed, but no one heard the thief come in the night; sneaking into the camp and whispering away Urion without a sound or much sign of a struggle. All they could tell from the blood trail was that he had likely been grabbed by the throat stifling any scream and puncturing his carotid arteries. He seemed to have bled out before he had been dragged even twenty feet. It was a staggering discovery that left them reeling in shock and dismay when they wakened, unable to believe what had transpired. Again, the police had to be called in and this did not bode well considering their last encounter. They did not dare to investigate this themselves for fear of being accused of tampering with evidence.

The police were not impressed that this group of men were again involved in a possible homicide in the same area as before. All of them with tracking and hunting expertise and the meat from the hunt not even touched by the assumed animal that could have been responsible for this death. Whether man or animal it had to be insanely large to drag Urion away leaving only heel marks and a blood trail. The police kept looking at Persæus with his incredible size and muscular build and even he had to question if possibly his demons had somehow manifested themselves during the night. They found what was left of Urion a full half kilometer from the camp, dragged through dense undergrowth and torn apart, mostly stripped of muscle.

It was obviously an animal of some sort but nothing like this had ever been seen by the police or the zoologist brought in to analyze the remains. What was left of the throat showed apparent puncture wounds that resembled a clawed grip more than a bight from teeth. It was most disconcerting for Persæus and Achilles knowing what he could become but his demons denied any involvement to Persæus which he had to accept. Not because they wouldn't lie, but because he had them shackled in his mind and he knew they could do nothing without his expressed permission, even if he was drunk and asleep. Still, the thought of being responsible for the loss of a good man haunted Persæus and he, more than anyone, wanted to get to the bottom of what had happened. The police wanted them to stay for the time being until the crime scene could be fully investigated and this time Persæus and Achilles did not argue. At least it didn't take long as the scene was fresh and there was little to go on, only the condition of the remains which didn't lend themselves to very much analysis; and paw marks.

They did find large paw marks in the dirt around the body but the zoologist could not begin to determine by what they had been made. Movement around the camp had obliterated anything around the point of the kill so this discovery had to be preserved. He made plaster castings and said he would have them analyzed by those that had greater knowledge of carnivorous beasts. They were the size of an elephant print and the animal had to be very dense in weight as they were several centimeters deep. The claw marks indicated it was not a cat as they did not appear to be retractable. The Zoologist estimated the animal had to weigh close to a half metric ton at the very least. And the longer they stayed in the area, the more danger they would be in, especially with the meat hanging in the branches above. The scent would keep the animal coming back but with pray laying on the ground it didn't try to get into the branches. The discovery of the paw prints vindicated the men as far as the police were concerned. The police allowed them to load the truck for the drive back to the city and by the time the investigation was done the entire combined group hightailed it out of the area, no one wanted an instant repeat that next night.

Persæus and Achilles didn't discuss their concerns with each other until they had dropped everyone at their respective destinations and returned the rental truck. They sat in the office and Persæus admitted his discussions with the entities but denied there was any possibility they had been responsible.

"I just don't see how they could get free of my control and do this on their own."

"Once upon a time they controlled you completely, is there no way they could do that again?"

Even Zeus put in his two cents, "No, I can't see how they could do that without Persæus' knowledge, Achilles. He would have to be awake and call upon them."

"Thank you, father. I appreciate your agreement on this."

"By the way, have you named them yet?"

Persæus was a bit embarrassed as he had actually done so, like the pets he now considered them to be. "Yes, father. They don't like my names for them but the names have a positive connotation. I call them Angel and Rover."

"Zeus laughed out loud with Achilles and he decided to appear physically. I'll bet they don't like that much."

"Well… not much, but I told them it was the only way we could have discussions so they accepted."

"Does Rover roll over and fetch? Do you tell Angel you'll buy if he flies?"

Achilles was rolling with laughter and even Angel and Rover couldn't get upset. Persæus thanked them for keeping a good attitude and he smiled at his father's humor. "You are terrible! You know that, don't you?"

"Yes, but I'm funny."

"No, I wouldn't demean them like that but maybe I can use those in the future if they get out of line. They have been good company for me some nights when I lay awake and they are cooperating."

"The point is, you are not responsible for what happened out in the woods last night. Don't beat yourself up because Angel and Rover," Zeus laughed again, "are not responsible and neither are you."

"But who or what is? We can't just forget that a friend and employee was killed and eaten by something demonic and that we slept right through it."

Rover spoke up through Persæus shocking Achilles, "I think I know. Oh, master and all-knowing Zeus, did you not give life back to Nyctimus and was he not brought back to life after you transformed Lycæus?"

"Yes, what's your point, demon dog Rover?"

Persæus could feel Rover's discomfort with Zeus' disrespect.

"Is it possible that Lycæus, in retaliation and jealousy, infected Nyctimus to pervert the gift of life that you gave to him?"

"Yes, I suppose but I would know of such a thing."

"Isn't it strange that Set and Ba'al made a move on this venture and that when they found out that Persæus is your son and in charge of... Angel," Rover was having problems using the names that Persæus had insisted upon, "and myself a giant wolfen creature has attacked?"

"Hmmm, I understand what you're getting at, but how would I not know of this infection?"

"Oh, high god of Olympus; you are omniscient but Ba'al and Set are the high demons under Hades, they are also deceitful and powerful. Might it just happen they intended to deceive you and they caused you to forget or not even know?"

"I find that highly unlikely."

"But it is possible?"

"I suppose it is possible."

"And now the curse that has been passed down from father to son for eons is invoked to take revenge upon you in some manner. Since they found out about Persæus being your son and The Works being a bane to their existence, it would make sense."

"What if Rover is right, father? I sense no attempt at deceit from him. And it would make sense that Set and Ba'al would attack our men and our company in order to seek revenge upon you and also upon us for rejecting them. It was simply an unfortunate set of circumstances that brought us all together in this moment. But the murder of Urion was calculated and evil."

"Then I'd say we have a real problem."

"It might be worth considering, Zeus," said Achilles.

"You boys keep your heads on a swivel; this might only be starting. Thanks Rover."

"You are most welcome." Rover's phrase had not completely come from Persæus mouth when Zeus was already gone.

"Your father is rude."

"Give him a chance, he grows on you."

Rover growled but he had said his piece, Zeus had listened and he was satisfied.

"You are quite the ventriloquist getting that wolf to talk to your dad like that."

Persæus laughed, "Maybe I should take up a different profession."

"What utter humiliation," said Angel.

Achilles burst into laughter.

"Chill out, you guys. I think Achilles is going to have an aneurism from laughter."

"If we could only be that lucky," said Rover.

"Watch it now, that's my cousin."

Uproarious laughter in three voices came from Persæus mouth and Achilles doubled over in laughter thinking, "This is going to be a trip!"

They all laughed out loud again when Zeus chimed in, "Oy Vey! What have I done!"

The night was wearing on and it was time to close things down and go to their respective homes. The boys had to process their kills the next day and Persæus really wanted to chat with his mother about the whole debacle. He was going to have to tell her about Angel and Rover; something he had hoped to keep secret for a time more. But it would have to happen sooner or later anyway. Besides, that part of the story was just too much fun to leave out and he couldn't do that. Danaë was devastated hearing about Urion. She knew he didn't have a family but for his father, still that would destroy him. Children know their parents will eventually die but a parent never expects to lose their child. She brought up an interesting point the men had not discussed, if this was indeed a creature sent by Ba'al and Set, how did it know where to find them?

"Mother, we never even thought of that, and could it be following us here?"

"We need to keep that in mind, we have to assume it will come after us all sooner or later."

"I'm wondering why it didn't take Achilles or myself. It would certainly have more of a direct impact on everyone."

"But it probably knows from Ba'al and Set that you are blessed with your entities and that makes you a hard target. Achilles not so much but he is also a god and the men with you were not. Their demise might cause you pain as you try to stave off this thing, this monster that is trying to haunt you. To haunt Zeus also."

"I wonder if we could set a trap for it somehow. I don't want to just sit and wait for it. Sitting on a game trail is just fine with timid creatures like deer, but this one is tantamount to a rogue man-eating tiger. For that type of animal, one needs a goat or other prey to entice the animal to hunt in a manner that it might not otherwise do."

"I just wonder if it is aware of its own ability to transform."

"I'm sure it is, mother. Even when I could do nothing about it, I was aware of Angel and Rover."

"Then it might be complicit in its crimes and maybe even enjoying the power it feels upon exercising the transformation."

"That would probably be true. I know that the few times that I have transformed I was drunk with the power of my demons and it was sheer joy; in great part because they enjoy their freedom when it comes around."

"Almost like a conjugal visit," said Angel.

Danaë was shocked at the voice coming from her son's mouth as he had never let her hear it before.

"And your father knew you were speaking with your demons?"

"Yes, he guided me such that I would not succumb to any temptations."

"He and I may need to have a discussion on that point."

"I wonder, mother; are there any indications that my sister might have similar gifts?"

"I can tell that she is special but beyond that, I don't know."

"At least I can protect her and help guide her as Achilles did for me."

"Yes, we should always be grateful for Achilles involvement in your life."

"Let's remember to speak with Achilles on Tuesday when we resume work."

"Let's invite him over for dinner tomorrow night and discuss it all then, son."

"Yes, mother. I'll let him know before I start processing the meat tomorrow."

Persæus did not have anything to drink that evening as he had consumed plenty over the weekend. Besides that, he wanted to be fully aware in case the Lycan found them in haste and tried to harm his mother and sister. He fully expected it to strike elsewhere in order to affect a more drawn-out scenario, but he didn't want to take any chances.

It was a cool evening and Persæus enjoyed sitting on the back porch for a bit before retiring. The sky was clear and the air was fresh and without any smoke from fires although the barbeques had been going strong earlier in the evening.

"It's here Persæus," said Rover, "and it knows I know it's here."

"Seriously? How can that be?"

"It's large and it's fast and it made it into town already. It's watching you right now, just beyond the next house from the shadows."

"Then I should be able to see its eyes." Persæus looked intently but he could see nothing.

"It's gone now, I don't know where it went, but it knew you were looking and it left. It may have been in human form that you didn't see its eyes."

"Is there any way to know it's human form if it comes around?"

"I can tell and I'll let you know."

"You're sure it has gone?"

"Yes, I can keep watch while you sleep."

"Thank you, Rover."

"Well, if you die, we die and we don't want to die. Wait, you can't die, can you?"

"I don't think so, but I don't want to find out."

"Good point."

Persæus slept knowing that rover and Angel would keep watch.

CHAPTER SEVEN: THE MAKING OF A HERO

Danaë was up before Persæus making breakfast and coffee and he told her of Rover's warning the night before. Of course, she was seriously concerned and did not want to be alone. When breakfast was done, she quickly changed so that she could go with Persæus to Achilles home not only out of fear for herself and her daughter, but also to check to see that Achilles was not harmed. They both wondered how it might have known where to find Persæus but were at a loss, except the possibly it perceived Rover just as Rover had known it was around. They got to Achilles home and he had a pot of coffee and bacon hot and crispy waiting for them.

"I felt it also, he said when they greeted him with their concern. The alcohol must have dulled my senses the night Urion died. I hoped you were going to come over this morning and I simply had not called you yet. It is highly malicious; I could feel the hatred seething from its very pores. It won't be hard to spot if it comes around while we are awake and alert."

"How do you feel about being here alone today, would you care to come over and process your kill at our home?"

"I don't know that it's necessary but I think it would be wise. It's intent and capabilities are well established and the only thing stopping it right now is probably daylight."

"Do you think we should warn the other men and Isis?"

"I don't think it will know where to find them. Isis maybe but it probably doesn't know of her so, Danaë, would you call her this morning and fill her in? Just in case and let her know not to go into the shop today. The phones can wait."

"Of course."

Achilles was in the habit of letting Danaë communicate with Isis as it seemed the proper way to do things with a beautiful, single young woman. It also established the pecking order between them although he doubted that was an issue. Isis had adapted well to working in the male rich environment although putting her in the third warehouse away from them all, likely contributed to that. Probably more for keeping the men away from her than anything. Even Persæus minded his P's and Q's, but Achilles attributed that to his mother's presence. Her being in the third warehouse now posed a problem they could not have foreseen with the beast out there looking to kill possibly all of them. They had to protect their people above and beyond anything else, the business was not the number one priority as it might be with other business people.

Danaë returned from her phone call with Isis and reported that Isis had felt something creepy when she had risen in the night, but it was not strong and only fleeting. It was gone before she had realized it was not good and in retrospect it may not have been about her at all. It may have only been a passing intent without a perception of her actual presence. The report was encouraging and they were glad she had such a clear perception of what had occurred. They sat for a bit enjoying the coffee before they packed up Achilles kill and tools for processing it. Danaë suggested he pack a change of clothes and stay the night with them as well. He locked his place and they walked the two blocks in between their homes and arrived in good time.

"We are being watched," said Achilles.

"I concur," Chimed in Rover in his low, rumbling voice.

Danaë looked at Persæus and just shook her head. She wasn't sure she would be getting used to that anytime soon.

They took a good long look around outside and didn't see anything out of the ordinary. There was however a man on a roof checking tiles that seemed to be in good order. Something about that caught Danaë's attention but when she went to point it out, he was gone; and so was the feeling of being watched. They went into the house and put the work they'd brought with them on the back porch. The boys got busy with that chore and had the meat done in only a couple of hours. They proceeded to sit around the kitchen table and discussed what had transpired that morning and also what they might do to trap and kill this creature that so obviously had malintent for them. If they'd had time to prepare, they might have utilized a reel of cable they had at the shop to make nets to suspend from the rafters at work but whatever they did right now had to be on the fly. Their plans kept coming back to Persæus, Angel and Rover and the probability they would have to take this creature to the woodshed and teach it a lesson; more likely the guillotine.

"You were right, Rover," came Zeus' voice, it is a descendant of King Lycæus' son Nyctimus.
Rover was pleased he'd been able to help and said so.
"I can't imagine how they got that over on me but I cornered Set and got him to tell the truth. By the way, Set won't be causing any more problems; permanently."
"What did you do, father?"
"Let's just say his place in Hades' realm is guaranteed. Did you know that Hades is gay? That's a recent development. I hope Set enjoys his company."
"Father, what did you do?"
"Oh, nothing much, but Set is likely hoping hell will freeze over sometime soon. Yes, you're correct, you'll have to battle this vile creature, Persæus." Said Zeus, changing the subject. "I'm sorry I have no better news but I've been away on this situation the whole time and there isn't much else you can do at this point."
"What about you, father? Can't you do anything?"
"Well, I could, but then what would you learn from it?"
And he was gone again.
Danaë commented, "I sometimes hate that man."

"God," came Zeus' voice.

"Whatever! I need a drink. Will you boys join me? I don't want to be the only alcoholic in the room."

Danaë managed to lighten the mood with that and they poured some of the almond liquor that Zeus liked. Danaë called out, "You don't get any!" and the bottle drained by itself.

"You are infuriating!"

"I gave you another bottle. It's in the cupboard"

"Thank you, Darling!"

And the boys and demons started understanding why Zeus and Danaë had been together so long.

At that point Persæus wanted to go find the creature and simply deal with it, but had no clue how to find it. Angel suggested they just do as it had apparently been doing and walk around.

"It seems to me that it probably climbed up high and simply searched the two of you out. With our heightened perception, we should be able to do the same thing. I mean, if that's what you really want to do? Single combat. Well, not really single you've got us."

"And me! Maybe after a few more drinks," said Achilles.

They laughed but Danaë was quick to point out that it would be best just to become the aggressors and go look immediately. It wouldn't be expecting that. So far, they had been playing nothing but defense. It was time to turn the table and play straight offense. Angel and Rover agreed, after all they were born to hunt and they were getting tired of this cowardly sitting in the back seat stuff. Persæus agreed and they downed one more shot for courage and headed for the church belltower. Achilles grabbed a couple of his long butcher knives and they walked tall going down the sidewalk and everyone moved out of their way.

They had to wonder if this is exactly what the creature had done right down to knocking on the church door. They got their answer when the priest didn't answer and walking in, they found him decapitated on the Narthex floor. The reverse collar had not stopped the claw that did this. The blood was mostly dried and they assumed it had been yesterday sometime. They climbed the stairs to the bell tower and Persæus and Achilles immediately felt it's gaze upon them. It was aware they were looking for it and that shocked it. That was not expected. They saw the same man Danaë had seen that morning, she recognized his shirt and when he noticed her looking, he jumped from the roof he was on, down to the street. They'd found him, but would he be in that same place if they tried to catch up to him? They decided to wait and try again later. They hunkered down below the rail to hide out and hoped it would lose them if they didn't show themselves. They waited until they felt the presence again. This time it seemed a bit stronger and they felt he was searching them out as well. It was now a game of cat and mouse. He knew where to find them and they had a good Idea how to find him. They took one more, good long hard look and spotted him walking toward the church. They descended the bell tower. The moment of truth would quickly arrive and they wanted to be on level, flat ground; not caught in a stairwell.

They stepped into the Narthex and then out the front door into the sunlight. It blinded them somewhat for just a moment and that was a frightening moment, indeed. Their vision cleared just as their subject rounded the corner a block and a half down and started to run toward them. He was stripping off his clothes so it was obvious he thought he would need them when this was over and that exuded confidence in his outcome. Persæus, Angel and Rover didn't agree, especially with Achilles support in the matter.
"Stay back, mother. You can't help in this; you are a witness for posterity."
The perpetrator's ears and arms grew and he started bounding on all fours, it was an awful sight to see as he transformed into a beast like Persæus. Persæus did not wait for the last second but brought himself to the full glory that Angel and Rover provided. Even though he'd seen it before, even Achilles was in awe as the

beast came to a screeching halt in obvious contemplation of the winged monster before him. The beast considered the monster and the monster eyed the beast and laughed.

"You are big Lycan but you are no match for us!"

The beast only snarled and they didn't know whether or not it had understood them.

It obviously knew there was something different about the three in one entity before it as it started circling as animals often do before they attack. It had a thought process as it showed caution before the monster that it had not expected to encounter.

"I have come to bring vengeance upon Persæus, son of Zeus, purveyor of lies and vile punishments for those over whom he rules."

"Then you have made a fatal error because you have found us!"

With that the three launched themselves at the beast, wings spread wide and howling so loudly the bell in the tower reverberated. The monster was indeed more powerful than it had ever been and the beast was taken back as the full weight of three meters of muscle and sinew impacted it. The Beast was large and it was no slouch but it was not prepared for the full-on violence of the attack.

Townspeople emerged horrified from their domains in awe of the spectacle unfolding before them. Staying well back but drawn closer to see these great animals slashing and bighting and throwing each other against the walls of the houses lining the street. The monster flapping its great wings and lifting the beast high into the air. Just to drop it crashing to the asphalt, bricks and concrete to lay for only a moment before jumping high into the air to grab at the monster's feet. It was a horrible sight to see and the fear ran deep in the spectators that could not turn their eyes away, horrified and entranced at the same time. Rolling over and over as one giant mass the two slashed and bit and howled and it seemed there was no defined winner as the minutes ticked by.

Then it seemed there was a pause as the two breathed hard and that's when Achilles jumped in with his sword sized butcher knife and slashed the beast's tendon just above the heel. It writhed in pain as it realized it would likely die. It knew it could not recover from this wound in time to eke out a victory. The beast felt the fear grow within and it showed in its eyes as the monster paused to give a victory howl to Zeus and the heavens. Just then, one powerful slash with its claws extended in full took the head from the beast's shoulders and sent it flying into the next block bouncing down the street blood splattering everywhere. Onlookers scattering to avoid being hit by the projectile and the blood. Its body laid in the street lifeless, the monster returned to being Persæus and the beast returned to the man he had previously been. The murmur of the crowd around them caught their attention at that point and they realized the spectacle they must have provided.

Danaë called out, "Zeus, Darling! Cleanup on aisle 6?"
Without another word the remains of the beast disappeared along with the blood on the walls and the people dispersed, some asking what had happened as though they had not seen a thing. That was the nice thing about being the consort of the high god of Olympus. Of course, her first concern was Persæus as he had sustained a lot of damage from the beast, but the bleeding had already stopped and he seemed to recover from the pain and the effort even faster.
"Thank you, Achilles, I did not see an advantage against the beast and was afraid it could go on for quite some time."
"I expected you might be evenly matched, but I thought that dropping him from above was a stellar move. I couldn't imagine him surviving such a drop but I guess his inner demon was as strong as your own."
Angel responded, "Oh, we would have taken him eventually even without you, Achilles, but he was very powerful indeed; your help was greatly appreciated. He was an older spirit and he was

very strong and it could have gone on a lot longer."

Danaë said, "Let me call Isis and let her know the danger is past, I don't want her worrying any longer than necessary."

Danaë stepped aside and started walking toward home as she spoke on her cell phone with Isis and the boys fell into line behind her. It was funny to eaves drop on Danaë's conversation with Isis as she was providing a blow-by-blow recount of the entire adventure from the time they had invited Achilles to stay the night. Men of course, would suffice it to call and say, "Okay, we got him. Goodbye," and be done with it. But Danaë spoke with Isis until they were all seated around the kitchen table and Persæus had poured another cup of coffee for each of them. This time he added a shot of mint liquor and Danaë called out to Zeus to see if he would join them.

"Well, I see that you dispatched Gregor without incident," said Zeus when he popped in. "Does mine also have the mint?"

"Of course, darling."

"Thank you, my dear."

"So, tell me, father, what lesson was this supposed to teach us?"

"Truly son, think about it. You, of course, the only one that had a ghost of a chance in single combat, but Achilles saw an opportunity to step in and shorten the fight before it had proceeded too long. It was a lesson in not only the importance of your individual roles but in the discission making that makes for battle ready team work. As long as you have been a team in life you have done well in business discissions, but you've never had the opportunity to enter battle together. I'm truly proud of you both."

"Zeus, did you see when Persæus picked him up and dropped him from on high?" asked Achilles.

"Hey," said Angel, "I had a little something to do with that."

They laughed and had to agree, "Yes, I saw the entire thing. You don't think I'd leave you to such an important moment alone, do You?"

The conversation continued for a bit and Zeus had a second

cup of mint coffee with them, unusual for him but he seemed as worked up over the victory as the rest of them. Then in a moment, he said, "We are going to make that mint coffee a regular thing on Olympus," and, in usual fashion, he was gone.

Achilles determined to stay the night even though their task was complete, he was still a bit shaken and if Persæus had been queried, he'd have admitted that he also had a bit of anxiety over what had transpired. Danaë admitted that she was happy they would all be together after their adventure and she suggested they enjoy a bit more alcohol to calm their nerves. They couldn't be full on drunks that night because of work come morning but it would be good to relax together and have the company. They had never been much into television but that night there was a 1957 classic named, 'I was a teenage werewolf' playing that starred Michael Landon. Between the hokey script and the alcohol, they howled in laughter. Of course, it lost a bit being translated into Greek from English but that's also part of what made it funny. By the time they retired, Persæus wounds were closed and beginning to disappear, except for the very worst of them and those might be mostly gone by morning. His healing properties were amazing but some of the deeper wounds would still take time.

When they arrived at work that morning Isis was already unlocking the door and turning off the alarm. She had needed that authority when they went hunting and she was to answer phones. She directed much of her conversation to Danaë but it was obvious she was manifesting a bit of hero worship for Persæus and he was eating it up. She was extraordinarily beautiful after all and how was a young man to avoid the praise of a gorgeous young woman. Danaë and Achilles both gave each other a sideways look as they noticed the intensified attraction between the two. The work day had to start and the adults in the room made sure the two had plenty to do to keep them out of each other's hair. The other men came in and those that had not gone on the hunt were informed of Urion's demise. It was promised they would close the shop for his memorial service and interment as they had for Niccoli.

A & N The Works Location Two was on the phone quite a bit that morning as no one had been available the previous day and the news was passed along to them as well, simply as a courtesy.

They Went about their daily duties and made sure they had properly covered everything on the schedule the week before. It never went over well with the customers when they made mistakes due to special occasions or oversights. That afternoon they got a call from one of their competitors inquiring if they might want to acquire their business. It was completely unexpected as the competitor was doing well enough in spite of the growth experienced by The Works. It seemed the owner wanted to retire and his family had done well enough through his life that they were not interested in sustaining the business; selling had been arrived upon as the solution. Achilles had to consult with Persæus, Danaë and even Zeus on this discission as the second location had taken quite a bit of their reserve capital. It would not break the bank but he felt inclined to seek the council of many before jumping into this. Of course, Leon and Joseph were involved in an important decision like this. The group had become an impromptu board of directors.

He called a meeting requesting Zeus attend in person; requesting, mind you. Zeus seemed hesitant and rsvp'd that he would try; typical Zeus. He was after all, a busy god. Achilles had Danaë do a quick work up of their assets and debts to be sure the numbers were current and they decided to meet at the home of Persæus and Danaë. They had started involving Isis in important meetings on a regular basis as she often had a good perspective on business discissions and she and Danaë always brightened up a room. Especially after they'd had a few cocktails, Isis was becoming family. More importantly, large decisions had an effect on shipping and scheduling so the two women needed to be kept informed and help make said discissions. They had come a long way since buying Alex' business the satellite shop had taken on several accounts and become quite busy and an integral part of the business. Achilles wished Alex could be there with them for the meeting but he decided that if his input was needed, he would conference call him.

The business reserves were coming back nicely but had not reached prepurchase levels and although the progress was good, it was not quite what Achilles had hoped. The Works still had plenty of room in the three warehouses and didn't need a new location in the same town. If they decided to buy the competitor's business, they would only be getting the customer base and income as an asset, the warehouse would be a drain on their income in upkeep and taxes.

"Do we have a possible buyer for the warehouse?" came Danaë's query from the kitchen as she prepared black olives, bread and olive oil as a snack for the guests. Persæus opened a couple of bottles of wine which were drained on the first pouring and had to be replaced with two more at the table.

"I don't know at this point," responded Achilles. "I have a couple of people in mind and a realtor looking into it."

Danaë was on top of this idea, "I think we should see if we can line up a sale of the property before we purchase the business, if that's our decision."

The others nodded and voiced agreement with the proposal. Angel and Rover were quiet as they seldom had any relative input on these matters. And then Rover piped up in his unique humor, "Eat the owner and take the business."

The table erupted in laughter and after things calmed, Isis commented, "Well, that's a unique perspective." To which Rover chided, "Quiet, peanut gallery."

"Who asked you, Rover?" was Angel's defense of Isis.

Achilles shut them both up with a humorous, "Great, a company meeting complete with circus animals."

The levity was good as everyone was finally accepting the input of the 'circus animals' and they were coming into line with acceptable standards of behavior. It had taken years but Angel and Rover were integrating nicely with Persaus and strange as it was, he was enjoying their company in his head. The meeting continued with suggestions for accepting the work load to make sure it would be good fit with the existing aspects. It all seemed to be a good fit and so the plan was accepted to make the purchase contingent upon having a buyer for the warehouse lined up prior.

This was the first time the entire group had met in a private setting and the comradery was at a high. It was lamented that Zeus couldn't 'pop' in as was his usual behavior but he was a busy god after all. Then Rover asked, "What if Gregor was not the only lycan from the line of King Lycæus?"
The room went silent, it had not occurred to any of them prior to this that there might be more than one beast prowling for them.
"Rover, you're such a buzz kill," came Zeus comment when he entered the room.
"Zeus!" was the clammer of the group when he showed his face amongst them.
"I hope you still have on hand that fresh bottle of almond liquor I gave to you."

Danaë had been playing hostess most of the night so Persæus got up and brought out the bottle and shot glasses for everyone. Then grabbed a second bottle he had in the back of the cabinet as the first was not likely to last very long; Zeus could be a lush when it came to the almond liquor.
"If you want my two drachmas on the purchase, offer them half of what they are asking. They are not doing as well as they pretend."
"Umm, dad? We're on the Euro now…"
"I don't care. You humans change your currency as often as I change my shorts."
"Every couple thousand years then," came Angel.

To which everyone laughed.

"Well, I didn't come here to be insulted." Zeus said. "No, quite seriously, they're not doing terribly but the real reason the kids don't want the business is because it is just barely staying afloat. The warehouse is worth something but the customer base isn't that great. You've taken a lot of their business in the past two years although I don't think you're aware of that. I know it wasn't intentional but your business model is of a nature that you schedule and deliver far more consistently than they've been able."

"Do you think half is really a fair evaluation of their business?" asked Achilles.

"You will be buying a warehouse, for the most part. If they balk, tell them you know what their books look like already, that's why you don't need an accountant's opinion on the purchase. They'll wonder how you know, just tell them a little birdy told you, they'll get back to you with a counter offer. Just stick to your guns."

And then he was gone. They were all disappointed as they were undeniably beginning to enjoy his visits. He had been absent so often over the years it was truly fun that he was coming around more these days.

"That's not a comforting thought, it seems they wanted to use us like patsies to line their pockets," was Isis' comment to the revelation.

"That's an astute analysis," said Persæus. "I knew there was a reason we invited you to these meetings," he said teasingly.

Angel mentioned they still had to address the lycan issue, Gregor had been a surprise and they didn't need any more surprises. "I think we need a means of ferreting out any others that might pose a threat to ourselves or any other employees of the company."

Angel was right and they all realized he and Rover had brought up a very important and valid point regardless of the fact it was outside the scope of the meeting.

Isis volunteered to see if she could dig up a lineage for Gregor to Nyctimus that might shed some light on the matter. They needed to trace the matter to keep Ba'al from using the line of family for more dirty work.

The afternoon had turned to evening so Danaë and Persæus began preparing a meal of venison steaks, lamb and fish for the lot of them. It had been a good meeting and a good visit, there was no reason to end it now and Leon suggested a game of poker for the after-dinner entertainment to which everyone was open. The bonding experience of such times was priceless and they were inclined to pull harder for the company. Achilles realized this and encouraged these times as much as possible.

The next day at work they were all a bit hung over but it was a positive day as the negotiations with the competitor were quick, they wanted to close down their involvement with the father's business. He was ready to be done with it and he realized they had a person inside if they had the information they claimed. It seemed they were in good position to know what was going on and they were making an offer that was very fair what with understanding the company was actually on shaky ground. The competitor was willing to come down in price and Achilles realtor had found someone willing to buy the warehouse for nearly as much as they were paying for the entire business. It was looking like a done deal and they allowed it to go through, they absorbed the customer base and it was an easy peesy done deal. It was only a matter of waiting on all the paperwork that was required for such a purchase.

Upon contacting the customers and informing them of the change of address and phone number for the company, some were aware already of the possible change of ownership and were happy about it. They had been ready for a change, not for malintent but several had been feeling they might get better service from the larger company. It was a good change and A & N The Works was well accepted as the new supplier of parts for many of them. Isis was able to trace the lineage of Nyctimus down to Gregor and there were, indeed, several likely other lycanthropes she would be researching. It was a matter of checking for untimely deaths surrounding the family line and there were plenty of unsolved cases that she would be looking into. The Executive staff would need to be watching out for their people while Isis made a list of probable assassins. In the interim Achilles called a companywide meeting and spoke of the realization that there could be issues that were putting their lives in danger.

Persæus still felt personally responsible for Urion's death regardless of what anyone else said to him and he knew he would be tasked with tracking down the murderous lycans and determining if the rest held malice toward him or his father. Even if they didn't, he would need to keep track of them in order to be sure of their true intent. This had turned into a real sh!t show about which he could only be an unwilling participant. Not one of Peter Pan's happy thoughts. It had taken three days for some of his wounds to heal completely from his fight with Gregor. However, it was quite memorable.

Isis was able to find one of Nyctimus' descendants right there in town and Persæus almost dismissed it because there had been no contact with him and no strong connection with unsolved murders. Still, he needed to be sure so he went on the prowl to find the intent of the next beast. Isis had come up with an address and Persæus assumed he would feel the presence of the man as he grew near to him. But for this beast, that was not the case; possibly as he held no malice toward Persæus and Zeus or maybe the beast within was dormant. Persæus decided to spend a night of the full moon watching over the domicile of the local beast and then he came to understand the nature of the man within. He was living in the rectory of a small Christian church in a Catholic society and although his faith was somewhat different, it was true and strong. The second night of the full moon when the pull was the strongest, the man went out and found a flock in the nearby meadows that he fed upon. Persæus wasn't sure if it was intentional or just a case of happenstance but this was quite obviously not a malicious entity and he felt it was quite safe to cross him off the list.

The next in a long list of possibilities was in the next town over, which was nice as he didn't have to travel far. This one, however, had a slew of unsolved murders in the surrounding area and it concerned Persæus enough to ask Achilles to come with him. Achilles could hardly wait, he felt he was fulfilling a bargain with Zeus to help end a threat to he and to Persæus and he enjoyed the idea of keeping his end of the bargain. Achilles was truly a man of honor which he proved in the daily workings of his business and his friendships. Persæus loved his cousin for this reason above all others. Just being with his cousin was uplifting and endorsed Persæus' respect for Achilles. They found the residence of the beast in question just after nightfall and the moon was just coming over the horizon. It wasn't long before the beast in human form exited his door bidding his wife and child a good night. It was strange to see this behavior in the persona of a werewolf and Persæus had to consult Rover on the point.

"Wolves are actually quite family oriented; we have complex social behavior and are strongly territorial. Much of the reason I have become so attached to you since you have included Angel and myself in your family gatherings," confided Rover.
"And me, I'm just a slut," quipped Angel.
Persæus almost broke their cover he wanted so badly to laugh at that.
"Aren't all Nephilim?" asked Rover.
"Right, but don't hold it against me."

As they watched the beast come from within it was intriguing to watch as he hid from human after human that he didn't attack, nor did they seem to notice his presence as he hid from them. Until he came upon a man seeming to hide in the shadow of a doorway. Then the monster and Achilles felt the malice in the beast's heart and mind. It was on top of the man before they could even realize this was its intended victim. They jumped from their hiding spot and surprised the beast stopping its attack that had been efficient and quite deadly. It recoiled not understanding what it was facing as man and monster got between it and its meal for the night. Rover addressed the beast, "Why did you kill this human?"

The beast just stared and growled as though it had no understanding. It backed away and circled to an open spot before it darted away without explanation. The monster nearly ran after him but Achilles held him back, it was not necessary to chase after an animal that would come back to its kill.

They hid out, hoping the beast would not catch their scent and waited patiently. They didn't need to wait very long as the animal of the moon came slinking back, wary and quiet knowing it was likely being watched. They didn't jump or try to surprise the animal but rather stepped slowly into the light of the streetlamp making no sound even from their footfalls. It stopped dead and cocked its head to one side as though listening for an absent sound. "I want an answer, why did you kill this human?"

The beast replied this time, "He was an evil man that took advantage of children, the Earth did not need him anymore and I was free to dispatch him."

"Are you the only one of your kind here?" asked Rover.

"I am not aware of any brothers or sisters."

"So, you are responsible for all of the ghastly deaths in this town?"

"I believe they are most all to my pride."

"We are looking for the pack of Gregor, they are a danger to us."

"He is but a distant cousin and I have no truck with him or his kind, you will not find any of them here."

"Then if you will excuse us, we're sorry to have interrupted your hunt."

"At least tell me who you are that I may address you properly if we should meet again."

"I am Rover and Angel and we are of Persæus."

"I am Achilles, cousin to Persæus."

"I am Vengeance of Nico and I free evil souls to wander back to Hades."

At this point, Persæus transformed back to his human form, still on guard waiting for an attack that thankfully didn't happen.

"We will leave you to your work, then. It is not our business if you destroy evil. You may come and find us in the town of Phthia if ever you need friends to fight beside you."

With that the beast turned to the business of eating as it was more beast than human and that was more than Achilles and Persæus cared to witness; they were happy to walk away.

That was two of the many on their list that were of no consequence to them and they didn't mind crossing Nico off their list of predators; he was doing the world a favor. They did not have time to travel to the next town if they were to work the next day so they curtailed their search for the night. Unless any of the predators they sought were of a nature as Persæus, they had only one more night to seek out these descendants of Nyctimus and Lycæus before they would have to wait for the new cycle. Tomorrow night it would be the third moon, a new town and a new hunt, but the tell tail malice was a good indicator of who they sought and that made the hunt just a bit easier. They traveled back to Phthia and stopped at Persæus and Danaë's place where they found her and Isis having drinks over a small desert of Crème Brulé. Danaë had made extra in anticipation of the boy's return hoping to reward them for a job well done. Upon hearing their report, she was just as happy with the outcome as she would have been had they found an enemy and neither of them had to suffer any damage.

They had an enjoyable evening with the ladies and Persæus was beginning to feel as though his monster was a blessing as Zeus had suggested so many long years ago. He was thinking about how long it had actually been but in reality, it was as fresh in his mind as yesterday. It had become a blessing mostly as he had accepted his demons and invited them into his everyday thoughts. He wondered at times if this was their penance for the evil they had done in another life and how much they might actually be indebted to him for taking them into his heart. A heart that he was given to be very much like his mother and also the benevolent god that his father, the king of Olympus, was seeming to become. In the old days there were tails of Zeus being cruel and unforgiving yet today he was jovial, kind and even fun at times; not at all the way he had always been depicted. Persæus was thankful for that as he enjoyed him this way; much more than he might have in his previous format.

After Isis and Achilles left for their respective homes, Persæus helped Danaë clean up the few dishes they had and went to shower. He was not exhausted but minor fatigue seemed to be a normal state of being after he transformed and he was looking forward to the comfort of a good night's sleep. One more night of searching for the next culprit and he would be able to relax until the next cycle of the moon. He wondered if Angel and Rover felt the same way and they assured him they did. It was wearing on them as well and they looked forward to peace for a few nights. They would need to travel to Athens for this encounter.

Achilles and Persæus made their way to the train and traveled to Athens much as they had when they met with Alex. It was not a terribly long ride and they departed the train at the main station just as they had before. In fact, they noticed the address that Isis had provided was fairly near to the second location of A & N The Works which seemed especially disconcerting. The location seemed almost too convenient to be coincidence and Achilles made special note that there was no such thing as coincidence. Too often humans and gods overlooked the fact that their lives revolved around the same people and locations that are familiar to them, at least in part from habit and then too, from familiarity.

The sun was already down but this night the moon was late in rising. And they had to wait for a couple of hours. That would put them home late as well due to the train ride, which they didn't relish, but it was the nature of the game. There was a small pub across from the address that Isis had provided and they sufficed themselves to sit and nurse a beer until the moon rose. They felt the malice as soon as they entered the door. It was strong and it was definitely directed at them. Whoever the beast was, he was here, he knew them instinctively and he was watching them with deadly intent. Achilles decided to use the men's room and afterward he walked over to the old record machine which was playing the latest of hits. Tipped back on two legs of a chair sat a man next to the player that was watching every move that Achilles made, from walking, to turning on his heel to the swivel on which he kept his head. As Achilles approached the man tipped forward and stood up to walk away. Achilles was afraid the man might walk out the door so his eyes followed as much as he could without turning his head.

Persæus also noticed the interaction and the malicious feelings that seemed to follow Achilles around the room. The man sat at a table near to the door and ordered another drink as his eyes scanned the room. Persæus felt those eyes land upon him and with them the same malintent that had followed Achilles. The three knew without doubt who each of them was and how the night might possibly end for at least one of them. Achilles, always assertive, went and asked the man if he and his friend might sit with him; really ballsy of Achilles and Persæus had to admire him for making such a bold move. He rose immediately and walked over to the table to give the man little if any moment to refuse. The malice permeated the air and it hung heavy with murderous intent that was stifling and made Persæus almost sick from the stench of it. "We are here to stop you from causing any problems for us or those that we know," Achilles informed the man. His dark beard and long hair making him look more foreboding than most.

"You won't stop anything; you can't stop the three of us together and it's too late for you to kill one of us at a time."

They didn't know what the man meant until they realized two others had stepped up behind them. That was a horse of a different color, but it was still one that Angel and Rover assured Persæus they could ride. Persæus wasn't feeling that confident but his demons had not lied to him ever before, nor did he mistrust them now. Rover informed him the moon was beginning to rise and the men would be able to transform before much longer. A smile came across the first man's face as he asked, "Do you feel that? I do and it feels like power!"

The two behind laughed and the entire pub stopped to watch what was about to transpire although they had no clue the extent to which it would be far beyond their realm of belief.

Persæus got in his face, smiled and said in Rover's voice, "Why don't we step outside?" the man lost his antagonistic smile and looked a bit unsure of himself as he glanced at the other two.

Achilles laughed at the change in persona and turned to look at the two other men, "You're going down and it won't be pretty."

As the five of them stepped outside several of the humans within tried to follow them out and Achilles warned them that it would be very unwise. It wasn't as if they had never witnessed a fight before so they exited anyway and Achilles merely said, "Don't say I didn't warn you" as he pulled his knives from beneath his jacket. Persæus prolonged his transformation; first growing to three meters then allowing his claws, ears and teeth to grow and lastly, with a malevolent howl he blossomed his hair and wings together and his presence filled the entire width of the street. The men that had followed them out screamed in terror and tripped over each other trying to get back inside making Achilles laugh. The shock and awe on the faces of the three beasts as they started to transform was not overlooked by Achilles and Persæus and before they could turn, two were already in pieces beneath Persæus feat. The other languished at the end of Achilles knives, both piercing his heart and allowing him to pump his life's essence out of the front of his chest. Persæus removed the last beast's head for good measure. It was over almost before it started but it had been three against the boys and they took no chances nor any prisoners.

"Umm, dad… I hate to bother you, but…" and it was no more said than Zeus had cleaned up and made the witnesses forget.
"Service with a smile," came the voice in their heads and it felt good. "But why must you always be so public in your efforts?"
"You used to enjoy the gladiators, Zeus," said Achilles.
"Okay, point well taken. But next time you might consider a little bit of privacy?"
"Yes, sir," they both said together.
Persæus wasn't quite sure what difference it made as Zeus made everyone forget anyway, but it couldn't hurt to please the god over all of Olympus. They went back inside and had another beer as the interruption had allowed their first to go warm and flat.
The bar maid asked, "Anyone see what happened to Sabastian and his friends? They didn't pay for that round! That's going to come out of my pay!"
"They had to leave unceremoniously for other parts," said Persæus with a smile and Achilles knowing smirk. "I'll buy their drinks for them, it's the least I can do," which in fact, it was.
"By all the gods, boy. I think you take after me more and more," quipped Zeus.

They finished their drinks and started walking out the door when they bumped into Alex.
"Well, what are you gents doing here?"
"We were traveling through from Cairo, we were looking at a proposition from a manufacturer there that wanted to join our

group," covered Achilles.

"Really? And what did you decide, if I may ask?"

"They aren't big enough yet and You are good for us here in Athens. I don't think we need the extra paperwork. What brings you here?" He asked quickly changing the subject.

"Oh, my neighbor's son hired on with me today, he's tired of being a merchant marine. A young man named Sebastian. I wanted to come up here and have a drink with him."

"Oh, we ran into him. Seemed like a nice fellow but he and a couple of his friends headed for Cairo tonight. I wouldn't expect him to show up for work."

"Oh, dear. I was really hoping for some good help. Well, I'll put an ad in the paper. I'll walk with you boys back as far as my house."

As they said their goodbyes, they didn't notice any malicious intent from Alex' neighbor's place and they wondered if the infection had skipped a generation or if the neighbor was even at home. They might have to revisit the pub on a subsequent trip to visit with Alex. They proceeded to walk to the train station and conversed about the fight and how it wasn't planned to ambush the men, it just happened, it was like they were on the same wave length. "Possibly a lucky thing for us," said Persæus.

"Good men make their own luck," said Achilles.

Persæus supposed he was right. The train ride home was unremarkable and they said their goodbyes at the intersection as they so often had. They would continue their pursuit of the infected on the next cycle. For now, they could relax for a few weeks.

It was time for dinner but Persæus didn't really feel like eating, he'd had enough beer that he wasn't really hungry and Danaë had gone out with Isis anyway for a girl's night out. He didn't have many nights by himself and it was an odd feeling but he also felt the fatigue he normally did after transforming so he decided to get ready for bed early. He wanted a good night's sleep to start the next day fresh. But it was not to be. His dreams were turbid and full of negative feelings, he saw visions of giants, sea monsters and dragons his friends had all turned against him. He hated the feelings of rejection and loneliness. He tossed and turned and wakened not wanting to lay down again. Fear haunted him for no discernable reason and his heart palpitated as though it would burst from his chest. It was the worst night of sleep he had ever had and there didn't seem to be any cause except that the past several years of memories were all involved in one manner or another.

When the night was deepest, he was wide awake and had no desire to sleep. His mother had come home and Isis was sleeping on the couch so Persæus, getting a cup of coffee, stayed in the kitchen so as not to disturb her. But even so, she wakened and came to sit with him and he told her of the night in Athens, his fatigue and his awful dreams that scared him more than dealing with the beasts. There was no rhyme or reason to his dreams, visions and the feelings of fear and loneliness. But Isis did her best to comfort him for which he was grateful and they talked the rest of the night until the sunlight peaked through the windows. It was kind of Isis to spend that time with him as she lost sleep that she could have used. It would be a long day for them both but at least the shop was closed today as it was a Sunday.

Danaë was surprised when she rose to find the two of them talking but she didn't make mention of it. She started some breakfast as though it was any Sunday morning and Isis jumped in to help. The girls were planning on going shopping together and Persæus called up Achilles to see if he had any plans, he said he wanted to watch the football game and invited Persæus to come over for the afternoon. After the breakfast dishes were done Danaë was quick to spirit Isis out of the house as she felt that the two young people had spent more than enough time together. Persæus was deep in thought anyway as his night's trepidations had him trying to understand what had happened.

But soon he was on his way of over to Achilles home to enjoy the afternoon with his favorite cousin.

Real Madrid and Inter Milan were playing and it was promising to be an incredible game. Persæus gave Achilles a hard time for his tiny little twenty-eight-inch television; after all, he did own a good size company and he owed it to himself to be able to see what was going on. Achilles had always erred on the side of frugality which was really to his credit but Persæus wasn't having it. He said that he would buy it himself if he had to but Achilles was going to upgrade today before the game was to start. He just about dragged Achilles out to the store by his hair but Achilles was kicking and screaming the entire way. Sort of. He really did want a larger screen especially as football was coming into the finals for the season. He could always put the smaller screen in his bedroom as he didn't have a TV there.

Persæus talked old Cephus into taking his donkey cart so they wouldn't need to rent a truck or wait on delivery. What a sight that made and people that knew them laughed and waved as seven-foot Persæus, six-foot Achilles and five-foot Cephus rolled a sixty-inch TV back home in a donkey cart. It truly was comical to see. For his part in the adventure, they invited Cephus to watch the game with them. Although he had not watched the young man's game in many years he agreed as they were having such a good time together. The three of them managed to get the screen up on the wall just as the game was starting and Achilles got the wine flowing shortly thereafter and Persæus ordered pizza with a few more people in mind. Persæus called his mother and told her of the adventure and suggested that she and Isis stop in after they were done shopping.

It had been several weeks since Danaë had seen Cephus and he and Isis had not yet met. Achilles decided to give Joshua and Leon a call and they came over with their significant others. It was going to be a party!

The pizza arrived just as all the guests arrived so the timing was perfect and with that, Zeus popped in and gave them all flack that he had not been invited. Of course, they told him he was always welcome and they hadn't forgotten, they just hadn't gotten around to it quite yet. They knew his travel time was incredibly short.

"Nice job of covering your arses," he said. "I'll forgive you if you break out some of the almond liquor."

And so it was that the high god of Olympus got down with the little folk and ate pizza watching football; even Hollywood couldn't write a better script.

The afternoon passed quickly, almost too quickly and when it was over Zeus had stayed far longer than anyone could remember him doing so in the past. Of course, as the game ended, he popped out in the fashion to which everyone had become accustomed but no one minded as that had been an experience none had expected. The afternoon had been a success but folks had to go and continue their own lives and each went their own way. Persæus, Danaë and Isis helped Achilles clean up and soon they were on their own ways home as well. It was nice that no one lived too far from each other and they promised to do it again sometime soon. The way of the world had come to a point that most people could not afford to own cars, have garages and travel much, but that didn't bother anyone at A & N The Works as Achilles paid enough for his people to own pretty much whatever they wanted. However, everyone there was quite frugal for the most part and had no need of a vehicle most of the time. If they did, they simply borrowed one or rented it. Sometimes, too often, they just borrowed Old Cephus' donkey cart. He didn't mind and he really enjoyed the company when they stopped by.

Achilles had learned long ago that sharing the proceeds of his company kept his employees happy and loyal and he had almost never lost someone to a higher wage or better working conditions. When people took a job with Achilles it seemed they stayed forever. And he still made money hand over fist as his people worked hard for the benefit of the company that supported them. Something that most corporations had forgotten or purposely ignored for the sake of enriching the executives. And Achilles vault was filling steadily regardless. Zeus had kept his promise and taken care of him for helping Persæus and Danaë. He could never turn his back on Zeus and continued to enjoy communing with him whenever possible. Zeus had become a best friend after all these years.

There had been no recent murders in the town of Phthia, Athens or anywhere that might affect the family of The Works and Persæus consulted Rover and Angel on the matter as he was coming to respect their opinions very much. They had come around from being the vile and abhorrent creatures they once had been and he felt a need for their approval on many decisions he now made on a regular basis. This was one of those times and he sat with a cup of coffee that next morning and asked their opinion on the probability of there being more of the malicious lycan they needed to address.

"You would be well advised to seek them out and question them at the very least," confided Angel. "I know of the evil within such creatures especially if they have been put upon by Ba'al to hate you and hate your father. I mean, look at whom I have for a roommate?"

Rover complained "Now that's just not right, Angel... I know you haven't forgotten the deceit and hatred that once filled me Persæus. You know you had to work on my spirit for years to make me even a little trustworthy. And just being honest, I still think back to those three days of full moon when I first arrived in full freedom and wonder what I might have become on my own. Don't worry, I'm happy as we are, but the thought does cross my mind, I would be lying if I said otherwise. You have shown me that being honest is really a truly better way to live. I would not trust any lycan out there until you confront each and every one."

"I was hoping that was not your opinions but I suspected

nothing less. I hate having the weight of that responsibility upon my shoulders, on our shoulders, but it is decisively there and I'm glad to have the two of you to help me in this quest."

"My thought is that Zeus knew this day might come when King Lycæus' descendants would be put upon by someone to go after the ones he loves most. I'm sure that is why he gave us to each other. If Ba'al can turn them, Zeus needs them addressed and if they choose to go a more wholesome way, I believe it is only right to live and let live," said Angel.

"I wish that Zeus could just send Ba'al to Hades as he did Set," mourned Persæus. He hoped Set wouldn't sit down in comfort for centuries.

"I'm sure that he would if it wasn't that another god would come along and do the exact same thing. Besides, Ba'al is a god equal to Hades and Hades doesn't want him in the underworld, he might try to take over," said Rover. "It is just best for us to continue with the course we have taken and see it through to the end."

"So be it," said Persæus. "I'll just do what the voices in my head tell me to do."

Persæus spoke with Achilles about this conversation with his alter egos, he suspected Achilles would feel the same and he wanted his cousin's support in all decisions that might affect them personally and the business; it was only right to do so.

"We have dispatched four and dismissed two from the list of fourteen that Isis gave to us so that leaves eight more to go. We are nearly half way there. We can always hope the percentages hold out and only have to deal with four or five," was Achilles response.

Persæus liked the way he tried to make light of the several that were left to them at this point, it seemed to ease the burden. The three days of the full moon were just around the corner and it was going to be upon them quickly. The worst part was that these were real people with real lives and families and the actions they must take, the actions required of them, affected more than just the actors involved. And it took an emotional toll on Achilles, Persæus, Rover and Angel; all of them. Not to mention their loved ones.

Pavliani was the next location and a train ride was in order to get there. It was only a couple of hours away but the countryside between was exquisite and the ride was almost too short. Isis had two addresses there they would need to look into but they were almost ten kilometers apart. That was mostly a blessing as far as searching out the culprits as there shouldn't be any cross feed in the malice detection department and hopefully, the two wouldn't be working in tandem. The first stop they had chosen turned out to be a dairy farm with both goats and dairy cows which was a feat of major proportion all by itself. The two were seldom found on the same land but this family had chosen to do so and by the looks, they had been successful.

They had arrived at noon and couldn't wait until sunset to find out who the lycan might be, if at all, so they simply walked up to the farmer they saw near to the house and asked outright as there was no malice they could feel.
"Hello sir! I am Persæus, son of Zeus…"
And there it was, not malice but certainly an emotional response. Persæus knew they had the person of interest but was not sure that this man was a danger as the feelings were not the strong, malicious hatred he had sensed before with the others. Rather, it was more a shock and awe as the realization was put upon him.
"I am Homer, I hope that I can say that I'm pleased to meet you. I know who you are and why you have come here. I hope that we can part as friends when it is time for you to leave. Is that something we can discuss?"
Not exactly the response they had expected, "You obviously know more than we had expected and you certainly have a foreknowledge of our purpose," said Achilles.
"Word has spread of the other's demise since the last cycle of the moon, a pattern established, it has had time to circulate, you will

not have the element of surprise anymore."

Rover didn't speak out loud but Persæus heard him in his head, "Well, that just about sucks."

"You wish to be friends?" Achilles asked.

"That is my earnest desire, I have no interest in harming any of you or your father, Zeus. I am satisfied to live out my life here with my wife and children, they haven't been infected. My father was of a different mind and felt the hatred but he practiced animal husbandry instead to satisfy most of his urges as do I. I was brought up in a manner, blessings on my mother who still lives with us, to hunt animals during the cycle and this has served me well. My father on the other hand, although a man of ultimate peace, used his, shall we call it, influence, to manipulate the people of the area when he found it necessary. I do not practice his ways. Ba'al has no hold on me and we praise Zeus of Olympus and Lord Vishnu."

"That is quite a claim," said Rover in his most menacing voice.

Again, the emotional jump from Homer, but no malicious intent at all.

"What spirit speaks from within you?" queried Homer.

"My cousin has the counsel of many at his disposal," said Achilles, "they were once his demons and now they are his protectors and friends."

"I would invite you in to break bread with my family but I can't take the chance of my children seeing something that would give them nightmares or induce evil thoughts. They don't even know of my affliction. I have kept that secret from them that at my dear wife's behest as she loves me but doesn't want that influence upon our children."

Angel said out loud, "I believe him."

Again, Homer was surprised but stayed calm.

"I only ask that you go and leave us in peace."

Persæus stepped forward and shook the hand of Homer, followed by Achilles. They had the answer they needed here and there was no need to further disturb the man or his family he so obviously loved.

"Namaste," was Homer's parting word.

The men responded in kind as they knew of this greeting and its origin in peace.

They were very pleased with this revelation of Homer and determined to remember him in the future if ever they were in need of a man of peace in the area. It was intriguing to them that he had chosen the life that he had and it was pleasing to know that a beast could adopt such a lifestyle. They decided to walk to the next address, but in just a few kilometers, they were haling for a ride from a passerby. Some kind hearted gent gave them a lift to within a half kilometer of their destination. He offered to take them the rest of the way but they wanted to move in without raising concern or curiosity. They made it all the way to the front door before anyone noticed them.

The neighbor came walking over, "You probably won't find anyone at home, he ain't been around for a while."

"You know the man that lives here?"

"I did, when he was still coming around."

"Oh, why is he not coming around?" asked Achilles.

"Well, I'm pretty sure that's because Peter's dead."

"Dead?"

"Pretty sure."

"Pretty sure?" asked Achilles.

"Ya, pretty sure."

"Why do you say that?"

"Well, his body wasn't moving much when they carried him out to the coroner's van. Probably a pretty good indication."

They all three chuckled.

"So, how long is a while?" asked Persæus.

"That was a couple of months ago."

"Can you tell us about him?"

"I could, but that all depends on why you want to know."

"We really wanted to talk to him about an illness he had."

"He wasn't sick when he died. And he died of natural causes. So, I'm not sure what you mean by his illness."

"It was something that came upon him like an allergy."

"An allergy, I don't recall he had any allergies."

"May we ask what you know of him and his death?"

"He seemed to be a private kind of person but in the years that he lived here, we got to know each other on a first name basis. He was a pretty good guy, at least I thought so; some others weren't so fond of him for cause. I kind of imagine by your stature that's probably the illness, or maybe allergy about which you wanted to talk to him."

"What made it obvious?"

"You seem nice enough but I got the impression you're the warrior types. You walked in from a ways away, kind of sneaky like. You, young fella, being ten feet tall and your friend here having knives strapped to his back were pretty much tell tail signs. I wasn't afraid because you came here in broad daylight. Only men of good intent would walk straight in in the daylight; any one should appreciate that. Peter would probably have talked with you. He didn't much beat around the bush."

"Do you think he would have been honest with us?"

"Oh, more than likely, if you asked him a straight up question. He wasn't prone to lying."

"I take it people knew of his malady?" asked Achilles.

"Malady? Of what malady are you speaking?"

"I'll straight up tell you; will you be honest?"

I always am, most of the time, always, maybe."

"Did he suffer from lycanthropy?"

"I'm not sure I'd say he suffered, but he did have a shiny fur coat on occasion. Some of us knew, some suspected, others that weren't on his good side found out the hard way. The police had no doubt the day they came out here and shot the shit out of him, those F'n bastards!"

"Do you mind telling us how he died? The Police? His type isn't exactly easy to kill."

"Nope, I don't mind and nope, not easy to kill. He died of natural causes."

What do you mean natural causes? You said the police were involved."

"I suspect it had to do with the twenty or so bullet holes they finally put in his brain. It took them a while. They say it takes silver but I'm here to tell you, there's just some things from which even a werewolf can't recover. Like, most of the brain being missing from his skull, that's kind of detrimental to existence, even for a werewolf."

"But you said natural causes?"

"He had half a brain which is kind of unnatural but naturally, he didn't live through that. Natural causes. Was there a specific reason you wanted to talk to old Peter?"

"Old? We were not aware of his age. Did he have any children?" asked Achilles.

"Well now, you didn't answer my question. You answer mine and I'll answer yours. Fair enough?"

"Fair enough, Mr...."

"Just call me Abraham, young man"

"Okay, Abraham. We needed to know if he held any malice toward me or my cousin Persæus and our relatives and friends. There is a group of lycan that have been influenced negatively by Ba'al against Zeus and many of us that know Zeus."

"He certainly was no fan of Zeus; I can tell you that, but he never went out of his way to express anger or hatred. It was more of an agnostic kind of thing, if you know what I mean. Nope, no children of which I'm aware. Kind of stayed to himself most of the time; except for Sophia. He had a soft spot for that woman, she just made him happy."

"Well, thank you Abraham. You've been very helpful. We're just trying to protect our own and we needed to come out here and see what was up with Peter."

"Ya, I don't think you'll have any trouble with Peter, death kind of puts a stop to that situation and I doubt he had any kin. You might want to stop for a drink at the Wander Inn on your way through town. That fat old girl name of Sophia that tends bar there, she's been scratching a lot, like she's got flees or something; if you know what I mean. Just don't tell her I said so." With that Abraham turned and started walking slowly back to his own place and waved over his shoulder to them. "Nice meeting you fellas!"

"You too, Abraham," they called out.

They felt they needed to check out Sophia, they got the impression from Abraham that he was one to mind his own business unless something was really important. He wouldn't have said anything about Sophia if he didn't want them to pay close attention. The walk to town from Abraham's place was relatively short and they just walked as the traffic in the road was light that day. Their eyes had to adjust to the low light inside the Wander Inn and it took a moment to see where Sophia was. When their eyes made contact there was an immediate suspicion in the air but not malicious intent. It was strong enough to almost knock Persæus to his butt. This woman was not liking him much and he needed to get her settled down so they could talk. He did the only thing he could do and walked right up to her, he introduced himself and his cousin and told her straight up, they had originally come out to talk with Peter.

That didn't do anything to calm her down but Rover told him she was curious now. Curiosity can be a good thing and Persæus continued.

"Sophia, we spoke with Abraham, a good man as near as we can tell. He told us much of what we came here to find out, but we want to talk with you. If you could bring a strong ale to our table and maybe talk to us when you get the chance, we'd really appreciate it. We'll answer any questions you have and we hope you'll answer ours."

"Like what questions?"

"Hmm, like, are you pregnant?"

The wide-eyed surprise on her face answered that all by itself. The boys were sure she would come and talk with them.

"All right boys, I'm taking a ten-minute break, don't bother me and I'll treat you good when I get back."

Sophia came to their table with the ale and she sat with them, "How do you know these things? Nobody knows them except me."

"I am Persæus, son of Zues, I have within me the spirit of a Nephilim and a Lycan, I understand more about you and your progeny than do you. This man is Achilles a god of Olympus and we traveled here from Phthia to ensure Peter was not a threat to ourselves, Zeus or any of our friends and family. Ba'al has turned many lycan against us and we are finding those that have taken a side and dispatching them."

Achilles continued, "From what Abraham has told us, Peter was primarily a good man and he had no issue with Zeus so we just want to be sure you are of like mind. We don't need any little lycans coming after us in our sleep."

"I loved him, you know. Peter. You're right, in his heart of hearts he was a good man. A hurt man by what life had thrown at him, but a good man none the less. I do carry his child. No one knew that, I didn't think Abraham knew that. Did he tell you?"

"No, he suggested we might want to talk with you and we deduced it with the help of the spirits within Persæus," said Achilles.

"The police murdered him. I hate the chief of police, if anyone deserves the hatred of my child it's him, not you or yours or Zeus. You have nothing to fear from us. But the chief of police... Some day he will get what he deserves."

"We certainly understand and we are truly sorry for your loss," said Persæus.

"Thank you."

Rover spoke in almost a whisper to Sophia, "You will have a boy," She shrank from the voice. "He will be a good man as was his father and is his mother. He will care for you for the rest of your life and he will protect you from any ill will. I am the lycan within Persæus and I have spoken with your son in his mind. He has the desire to do good things as did his father. Guide him well and he will give you great pride and joy."

With that, Rover fell silent and Sophia rushed from the table in fear.

"I think that went as well as could be expected," said Angel. They laughed.

"Shut up," said Rover. They laughed again.

But he knew it was risky and he only hoped that he had helped. They drained their ales and Persæus left a €50.00 tip.

"You've got the hots for her?" asked Angel.

They all laughed again. In truth, she seemed like a good woman, Persæus hoped she would be a good mother.

When they had walked outside Achilles asked Rover, "I thought lycanthropy was an infection normally transferred by saliva?"

"Normally but once in a blue moon, so to speak, it can be inherited. I was surprised also and I wonder how Abraham knew?"

Achilles and Persæus looked at each other in a panic.

Achilles cried out, "I think we know!"

They ran back to Abraham's place. There on the porch was a gray-haired old wolf sitting in a chair. He got down in an arthritic manner and walked slowly away into the nearby field. They knew he was no problem; he knew they were no problem and it made them smile to think he had pulled the wool over their eyes. He had been very disarming but he seemed to tell the very basic truth and didn't really appear in his manor to have anything to hide. They proceeded to the train and went home for the night. This trip had been a success in their minds.

It was still early in the evening when they arrived home and Danaë was there with Isis in the office at A & N The Works. The boys had stopped by to check on things as was their habit although they trusted everyone to do their jobs and see to the running of the company in their absence. It was a sign of solidarity to come in and not ask any questions. If there were issues, those left in charge could tell them about it and then it would be handled. They called Joseph and Leon in to tell everyone about the day as it had been a truly good day. The uproarious laughter over Abraham brought attention from the men all over the shop and some of the men checked to see if everyone was okay. Just kidding of course, they wanted in on the secret but unfortunately this was one time the executive staff couldn't tell them. They hated keeping secrets from the employees, but even some of the good stuff had to be withheld.

The next day they traveled to Raches which was more on the water front than even Phthia. It also had two contacts but these seemed to be working together as there were murders of two or more at any time and they were especially brutal. Whatever was behind these killings was especially psychotic and vile and they needed to be ended in no uncertain terms. They probably should have seen to these earlier but they were new to this hero stuff and didn't have a clue about the order in which to accomplish their efforts. If there was a future to their efforts, they would try to take these nuances into consideration as it could save lives. They could only live and learn and it hinged greatly on how long they lived. One thing that made these beasts appear to work together was the proximity and the concentration of the murders. Competing entities would not abide with each other if they did not have a pact of some kind and the number of people at each scene made a singular animal almost impossible. As the Brits might say, "It was a bloody mess."

They walked to the epicenter of the melee hoping to feel the malice or to notice some kind of sign of the perpetrators that might point them in the right direction. They had nothing and it was frustrating as the last hunt had been so insanely successful and fulfilling. They spent their time walking from one end to the other, crisscrossing and checking alleyways to no avail. Pretending to be reporters they checked with the police to find out if there was a discernable pattern. It was as though the beasts knew of their presence and were avoiding them. Of course, Hindu Homer of Pavliani had told them they were now known and they'd lost the element of surprise. This seemed to be proving true tonight and they were losing heart. It would be a travesty if these vile enemies had a communications network and knew everything to expect from the four entities hunting them. Of course, they thought it was only two which was to the advantage of the hunters.

They finally stopped at a pub to have a gyro and an ale as their feet were beginning to feel like pancakes flopping on the cobble stones of this retro town. Persæus requested graviera cheese on his gyro which seemed odd to the waitress but he didn't care, it just sounded good tonight. As they were eating their well-deserved meal there were screams from the street and the two were compelled to put down their meal and run to the location. They were taken back at the fact that the animals they witnessed were in fact, four actual wolves and wolves don't attack people. At least, none had ever lived to tell the tail. These were large animals so they knew they were transformed humans but they had no similarities to real werewolves.

Persæus and Achilles waded in to the pack with no fear as they knew this couldn't be as it appeared. Achilles using his knives and Persæus only transforming his hands into the formidable weapons his claws made and within only thirty seconds the beasts were piles of convulsing hamburger with human faces. Unfortunately, the animals had killed several people and it was a most heinous and hideous scene. They had not heard of such a pack situation in all of the research done by Isis nor in any of the lore they had ever read. The boys knew if they stuck around, they would have a terrible mess to explain especially covered in blood and all the video phones that were documenting the travesty.

They both looked at each other and said almost simultaneously, "RUN!" It was a set up and they hadn't vocalized it but they both knew it. Somehow, someone was ready for them. They had not announced their destination that evening but the lycans of Ba'al knew where they would be and had set them up for failure. But this failure was not failure as they had killed beasts of the full moon, but they had convicted themselves as the murderers of humans by killing beasts, incapable of transforming completely. They still looked primarily human after death. The poor wolfen victims likely didn't even realize they would die that night. And they had been to the police station asking about the murders; they would be on the videos. They probably had a massive mess. They could only hope that somehow, the public would support their story of wolves but they knew the media would crucify them regardless. The newspapers and social media might give them their alibi if they happened to be sympathetic but the corporate shills would stifle the truth without concern for the fate of the true heroes of the situation. They had stopped the killers cold but they would be seen as murderers because the bodies of the wolves did not match up with true wolfen bodies. It hurt Persæus brain just to think about it. No matter what they did they were probably in a pickle of untenable proportions.

"Zeus! Can you get rid of the bodies for us?"

C**P! He had only one word for the situation and not wanting to be crude he simply closed his eyes and tried to relax. While everyone around him lost it. There were so many witnesses this time, they had not been able to pick the time and place. People had been screaming that these were wolves and they had it on their video phones; but who were they and where were they with the video evidence? It was one thing with the full-on beasts, no one believed it was more than a film production. But with the bodies having human form in the end, it was very questionable. It might be wiped from social media by the morning for violent content if they were lucky. Zeus did get rid of the wolf and human bodies as without a corps, a crime can't be proven leaving only the cell phone records to be of concern. He did what he could about wiping memory cards but many had been uploaded live and that had to be left to the media censors. Once they played on the media cites he could get them but that was on a one by one basis.

"You know boys, without the bodies you're probably going to be okay."

"What makes you think that, Zeus?" asked Achilles.

"AI and CGI will be blamed for the images. I took care of the video at the cop shop too. I'm really not sure what concerns you, just leave town now that the issue is behind you and don't come back until after it cools down. I mean, how many times have you visited Raches in the past? Not often, I'm sure."

Zeus was right, they probably were making mountains out of molehills. They simply had never had this situation in the past and it was highly disconcerting. They didn't even go back to the pub for their food as the notoriety would bring the cops that were already arriving down on their heads. They headed for the train station and grabbed some food from a street vendor along the way. It was nerve racking that things had turned out like this and if they ever had another situation that appeared it would turn out his way, they... But what could they have done differently? People had been dying and they couldn't stand around and do nothing. As they thought about it, they realized Zeus was probably right and they had nothing to worry about. If there was any investigation, surviving video would only show that they had rushed into a situation to stop the carnage. Modern society was too complex for Achilles with camera phones, internet uploads; he often longed for the days when one might say, "Murders? What murders? I have no idea."

There weren't that many people on the train back to Phthia but enough that they couldn't talk much about it and they both kept replaying in their minds what had happened. They really didn't have a choice in the matter and the next time they saw this pattern, maybe they wouldn't rush in, maybe the best thing to do for their own sakes was to just let it unfold and deal with the beasts after the carnage had ended. Truly, it wasn't like it was the first time it had happened in that area, that's what had alerted them to it in the first place. So many had died at one time on so many nights, it was obvious this group had been left to fend or themselves and they had no leadership or connection to their true selves. They had one more night left in this cycle and they agreed they would go as far the other direction from Phthia and Raches as they could to avoid being identified. They parted at the usual intersection and went to their respective homes for the night. They had calmed down on the train ride home and they both believed things would be just fine.

Persæus walked in the front door and his mother was highly agitated as she recognized the boys on the nightly news. Oy Vey! They had made the news! The video showing over and over was out of focus because it was night and appeared to be dirty camera lens, but Danaë could easily pick out her seven-foot son next to the handsome Achilles clearly battling and killing wolves on the streets of Raches. "Zeus! Help!" The video scrambled and the news caster was making an apology for technical difficulties but they knew this was not the end of it. Persæus called Achilles and told him what he'd seen on the news and Achilles turned on the new TV on his wall and saw it on another station in beautiful sixty-inch, LCD, 4K, high definition. Wasn't that just a kick in the eggs? It was as though someone had gut punched him. There was no doubt that anyone that knew them would certainly recognize them. Then Achilles station was apologizing for technical difficulties; at least Zeus was staying on top of the issue.

"A little wine, son?" asked Danaë.
"How about a tall gin and tonic?"
"I'll join you."
"Easy on the tonic, please."
Even though Zeus was taking care of the videos being broadcast, enough people were seeing them that Achilles and Persæus might be recognized. Zeus would be wiping memories of course and hopefully nothing would slip by, he was a god after all, but it was nerve racking.

"Mother, do you think this will blow over?"

"I'm sure your father will stay on top of it, he's pretty good at that. All we can do is deal with the fall out, if there is any. What happened tonight?"

"Just exactly what they showed on TV. We think it was a setup of some kind. Homer out there in Pavliani warned us that the word was out and we had been expected. I guess we should have put more weight to what he was saying. I'm pretty sure Abraham knew we were coming as well. He sure handled us like a pro when we arrived at Peter's home."

"No pregnant women with lycan babies left behind to tell the tail?"

"I certainly hope not. I'm going to go get showered and ready for bed. Let me get a refill and I'll nurse this until I fall out. Morning comes early if I can't sleep although his should help."

"Good night son, I'll be laying down soon myself."

"By the way, how's my sister doing?"

"Just fine son, she's resting comfortably."

"Good to know. Good night."

They had wiped out a threat but created another in the process, hopefully it would come to an end without incident.

CHAPTER EIGHT: FINISHING THE JOB

There were just a few left with which to deal and they had one more night this month when the moon was at its fullest. There was one and possibly two near Anavra and one in Thermopylæ Pass and with the heat that they had stirred up they might want to avoid the challenge of dealing with two. Thermopylae was as good a choice as any for location as well and it was traveling away from Raches, that was a very good thing. They headed out before the work day was done and although their many trips out before this had been raising eyebrows, those questions had been fully answered and no one asked why today. They'd have to mention that to Zeus, they didn't need their friends and employees knowing these things as it could create issues.

Lamia was the city near Thermopylæ Pass, the pass being most notable for the battle between King Xerxis the First and King Leonidas of Sparta. King Leonidas, reputed to having only three hundred men (it was more like 7000) had defended the narrow pass against King Xerxis the First and as many as 300,000 Persian warriors for three days until they were betrayed by Ephialtes. Ephialtes, wishing to gain favor with what he considered the winning team, revealed a hidden goat path around the pass the Persians used to attack the Greeks from Behind. You see, Thermopylæ Pass had its own secrets. Not only a secret back door, but a goat path back door to the back door. They had to wonder if by some long ago laid plan that they were looking for a descendant of Ephialtes or one of the Spartan warriors he had betrayed. They couldn't know and were only speculating as a matter of conversation. Regardless, it was a chance to visit a bit of Greek history and the hot springs after which it was named; Thermos regarding hot and Pylæ regarding gates.

The train stopped in Lamia and they had to hale a cab to get to Thermopylæ, it was a town of sorts itself but the location didn't lend itself to having a rail spur of its own. They arrived shortly before dusk and had time to get a meal at the museum dedicated to the battle that occurred so long ago. According to the information at the museum, King Leonidas was aware of the path behind his troops and had taken precautions by posting the necessary manpower to repel a flanking force. But Ephialtes knew of a goat path around the force on which he led the elite immortals of Xerxis which cut off the Greeks and surrounded them allowing the Persians access to flank King Leonidas and his men. There in the pass, they fought to the last man, brave but overwhelmed, they had managed to inflict incredible losses on the Persians. Due to overwhelming naval prowess and the addition of other forces, the Persians eventually lost and were driven from Greece. The Battle of Thermopylæ had proven the Persian forces could be defeated in spite of the battle being a loss for the Greeks. It inspired greatness and the carnage the Greeks visited upon the Persian forces could not be questioned.

The epitaph to the Spartan forces by the poet Simonides, reads: **Stranger, to the Spartans go, and tell that obedient to their orders here we fell.**

It gave them both pause to think about the fears they'd felt the night before, when it seemed they would be exposed and likely arrested. They took heart at the true bravery of King Leonidas and his men in doing what they knew had to be done to defend and repel, if possible, the invading forces that threatened the very existence of the Greek nation they loved and their own families. There is no record of what became of Ephialtes and it seemed he was lost to the dust of time as should be any traitor. With any justice from the gods, the cosmos or just existence itself, he would be suffering still for his betrayal.

As the sun was setting, they were inspired and determined to find the lycanthrope that seemed to be abiding here in the pass and determine its demise if necessary. Isis had pin pointed the area from reports of multiple horrendous murders that coincided with the cycle of the full moon. They could only assume at this point that it was lycanthropy and they were ready for that to be the case; but it wasn't. It wasn't even anything close to Lycanthropy and the truth would be stranger than fiction. It would break their hearts but it was a just punishment that needed to be ended. The Punishment was over and it was time to move on. They would be happy to have come here and helped in this situation. On their way to the museum, they had the cabby roll through the streets of the town which was only five blocks long and a few wide. Hardly a flash if one blinked going by on the freeway and they had noticed no indication of a werewolf. The moon was not yet up and they knew the impressions they would get would be growing stronger when it rose. Still, they did not distrust their senses, Persæus and Rover, so they opted to explore what was available of the pass itself.

The night was just perfect with the breeze coming off the ocean, balmy, in fact. They came to the pass of Thermopylæ and were in wonderment the Persians had boxed themselves into such a place with the Greeks. There were other options to get past but it seemed there must have been a reason for such a decision on Xerxis' part that seemed to escape logic. Maybe to get passed the inlets along the shoreline and to a main area of ocean where their ships would be waiting. It was certainly the perfect place for an ambush and slaughter. The night sky was covered with broken clouds and the moon shown bright only on occasion as those clouds passed by.

Achilles was enjoying the walk when Persæus suddenly turned

into Rover full on and without apparent cause. It scared him with its suddenness and strange bobbing and weaving he witnessed, claws flailing, wings flapping, teeth snapping; then it was over... Persæus was again himself and shaking his head, "Didn't you see that?"

"See what?"

"It was a great sea of men at battle, thousands and thousands, slicing and stabbing and dying without end."

"I saw nothing. Are you alright?"

"No, I don't think so. I didn't see you when they were present, be careful in case it happens again."

"Rover, can you tell us anything?" asked Persæus.

"I was stunned also, I have no idea what happened, but it was a great battle and we were not excluded. It seemed they wanted us as much as anyone on the battlefield."

And it happened again, in the blink of an eye they were in heated conflict fighting for their lives and Achilles was nowhere to be seen. One side was full of black-haired sun blackened men with helmets that covered only the tops of their heads; while the other side were bronze men whose helmets covered their noses and ears to below their jaws. The bronze men fought without fear but were being slaughtered from front and rear and Rover did his best to defend them while keeping himself alive. He knew that somehow, he was fighting the battle of Thermopylæ from almost 2500 years ago. Only as much as he fought for the bronze men, he was not on anyone's side, they all saw him as the enemy. And then he wasn't.

"Get me under the shadow of the pass, quickly!" said Persæus to Achilles who had reappeared.

"What did you see, cousin?"

"It was the battle of Thermopylæ and it was every bit as real as you are to me. I was still in Rover's form and although I fought for the Greeks, they still saw me as lycan and were fighting me in fear. I was defending them but they didn't realize it."

"How can that be? I saw nothing but you nearly took my head off."

"And if you happened to step into my way, I would. I wouldn't even know it but I would kill you succinctly and without compassion. I only saw Persians and Greeks."

"And now you know the fate of a traitor, to forever be embattled and lost to the world of men, only allowed to live while dying on the field of battle," said Ephialtes. There was only a shadow of a man in the partial moonlight at their feet, but the voice was most certainly coming from the shadow. It was not in full moon light and only a half of a profile showed from the waist up.

"Identify yourself, specter!" yelled Achilles.

"I am Ephialtes, I am cursed to suffer the battle night after night of the full moon and die many times over."

"But those dying from the lycan in this pass, surely that is not you?"

"I am not lycan but I am most assuredly the cause of innocent death, just as I was so many centuries ago. It is my fate and I am most heartily sorry for my transgressions."

"Are you truly that for which we are searching?"

"I believe that I likely am. From time to time an innocent might walk through here on the night of the full moon and they come under my sword. I try not to do it, I can no longer stomach the murder of innocence, but it is my lot in death and there is nothing which I can do to stop it. I am cursed to kill again and again and die on the battlefield over and over every night of the full moon."

"How is it we can talk to you and not die?" queried Persæus.

"You are standing in a place where I may join you if only just some of me exists in this world and the other in which the moon puts me, you are standing over my bones."

"So, if we move from this very spot?"

"You will not see or hear me."

"We are tasked with stopping these murders, is there a way to free you from this curse and stop our world from suffering the loss of life?" asked Achilles.

"You can, demi god Persæus, son of Zeus."

"What must I do, Ephialtes?"

"To free me from my curse you must dig up my skull from beneath your feet and throw it into the moon light…"

The clouds again moved over the moon and Ephialtes was no longer present. So, they dug up the skull from under their feet and did as he had requested. The moon was behind the clouds still, but when it finally appeared again it shown on the skull and they could see the full, opaque form of Ephialtes.

"Join me Pereus and let me proceed to the next world, I beg of you."

"As you wish."

Persæus stepped into the moonlight and Rover was there fully fighting for his life. But he could now fully see Ephialtes and there, with one mighty swipe of his clawed hand, he slew him without hesitation or question. When Persæus took the head from the apparition's shoulders, the skull flew from the moonlight against the surrounding rocks and shattered. Ephialtes was gone and released from his curse. The battle that Persæus could see disappeared, the din gone and Persæus returned to the real world.

"Well, that was trippy," said Angel.

"So observant of you," said Achilles.

"You expected something more poignant from a Nephilim, seriously?"

"No, I suppose not. Are you alright, Persæus?"

"Yes, I could feel his joy as he passed into the next world. It was truly good."

"Let's go home."

Persæus was pensive on the walk to the town and the cab ride to the train station but seemed to perk up as they boarded the train. They were the only ones leaving form Lamia at that moment and Persæus said to Achilles, "He really was truly happy. I can only imagine after fighting for so many months, so many years and so many centuries; killing and dying so many times knowing it might never end."

"He had been a traitor but the punishment seems to have changed him. I wonder to which realm he will be relegated?"

responded Achilles.

"Zeus?" asked Persæus.

"No, boys. It's best I not tell you his forever fate, a traitor's fate. It's not going to be pleasant, but he's in a far better place than he was and he's much happier than he was. Best just to leave it at that."

"Thank you, Zeus." They both said.

"You're very welcome. I thank you and he also thanks you."

"Next month, Anavra," said Persæus.

Over the next month they made the news a few more times than they would have liked, but Zeus had managed to rid the Media of the surviving videos. He had also taken care of the few memories that had certain knowledge of what had actually occurred in Raches. Persæus had wanted on a few occasions to go back to Pavliani to visit with Abraham, Sophia and Homer, but he thought better of it so as not to stir up any emotions. Rover suggested he not approach them unless there was a need, for everyone's good. It was better to leave well enough alone. The Works was running fine and they saw their profits rise from the new acquisition. As word got around that the competitor had sold out orders increased as companies determined they didn't want to second source the products they needed.

The other smaller fabrication shops started coming around to see if Achilles wanted to buy them out also. He didn't need the work but he still was not filling his now four warehouses, counting the second location in Athens. The private board of directors made up of the executive staff decided to buy up a few of the smaller companies, hire their people and use their locations for new enterprises. They associated themselves with the rest so as not to drive everyone out of business. That would not be good for anyone and the business model kept most people happy. The new enterprises were materials, parts and supplies for related industries which made A & N The Works very popular as they now, really were the works.

When the cycle of the full moon came around again, they knew they were likely up against a pair of lycans and they didn't want an instant replay of the previous disaster. Zeus kept telling them it wasn't a disaster but they felt otherwise. They decided to travel early in the day so they could scope out Anavra and see if there were any surprises awaiting them. Zeus didn't think they needed to do that but he didn't deter them either. To them, that was a sign he might know something he wasn't saying to them. A storm had blown in off the coast and they were soaked to the core when they boarded the train. They were not the only ones wet and the floor was soaked as well from all of the dripping passengers. It was good the temperature was down with the storm as all the water had the humidity high and the train smelled a bit like wet dog. They hoped that wasn't some kind of omen and Rover gave Persæus flak for that thought.
"Wet dogs don't smell bad; they just smell like... wet dogs."
"To each their own, Rover."
"Whatever."

When they arrived in Anavra they immediately felt malice from one end of town and they were shocked at how strong it was. They found a pub in the area that had a room to let and rented that for the night. After getting themselves set up they went downstairs to the quaint little place and ordered dinner and wine. The waitress came to the table in an agitated condition when she took their order and asked if they wanted an appetizer and something from the bar. Oddly, she kept looking toward the bar maid like she was worried about something. They ordered salted avo slices and a gimlet for each of them and when the waitress came back with the appetizer she whispered, "Don't drink the wine when your dinner arrives."
That was not a good sign and they both decided to take a bite or sip of any new items presented to them and then wait to see if there was a reaction; starting with the gimlets and avo slices. They tried to make lively conversation but the message from the

waitress had piqued their imaginations in ways that didn't allow for comfort or clarity of thought.

The next time that she came by to check on them she made a small spill such that she could justify a longer moment with them and she confided, "The owner is not your friend and he knows who you are. I would warn you to leave but that would look bad on me as well as you. Be forewarned, go to bed early and lock your door, move the dresser in front of it." She was gone again and she said nothing more the rest of the meal. When they failed to touch their wine the bar maid came by and asked if there was something wrong, Achilles said, "The gimlets affected us far more than we thought, you mix a good drink."
"Well, it seems a shame to waist a half carafe of wine but that's up to you boys."
"You are welcome to it if you wish," toyed Achilles.
"I'm not allowed to drink on the job, but I can have it delivered to your room if you wish?"
"That's an excellent thought," said Persæus, "Thank you!"
"I'll have it sent up now."
That seemed to please the bar maid and their waitress winked her approval on her way past. After all, they didn't want to stir up suspicion, not only for their own sake but for that of the waitress. It would not due to create a possibly deadly problem for the person that may have saved their lives.

They had both ordered the lamb chops with sautéed asparagus and fried baby red potatoes followed by leche flan. They took their time eating but it seemed the only thing that concerned the waitress had been the wine and they noticed no ill affect from any of the food. Because they had given time to each item on their plate to test for drugs of any kind, they finished later than they had expected and they went to their room around Eight Thirty. They were cautious entering the room but found nothing out of the ordinary and then they checked the window to see if that was a viable escape route. Being on the second floor they were surprised the window opened but also just as surprised to find a ledge on the outside. They did as the waitress had suggested and after double locking the door they moved the dresser in front of it. It was not a comfortable feeling knowing the situation was not as it appeared but at least they had knowledge of a possible situation. They poured the wine into the toilet rather than the sink and flushed it so that there wouldn't be even anything left in the sink drain trap, then they readied themselves for bed and tried to sleep. That wasn't going to happen, at least not much.

Around Two Thirty AM Persæus found himself asleep when Achilles shook his shoulder then put his finger to his lips indicating he should be quiet. Achilles carefully and quietly opened the windows to the ledge and motioned to Persæus they should go out. They could hear someone fiddling with the door and they weren't all that quiet. They climbed out on the ledge and waited. It wasn't so high that they couldn't jump down and Achilles handed Persæus a blade in case someone stuck their head out the window. The waiting was the hard part because whomever was trying not to waken the entire place, had no skills at cat burgling. They weren't getting the door open regardless of how long they tried. It seemed an interminable amount of time they stood on the ledge waiting and listening to the ineptitude of the criminals trying to break in. Finally, in apparent frustration, the door burst open and the dresser was laid waste on the floor. They could hear heavy breathing and upon realizing the two weren't in the room a low rumbling growl from not one or two, but three lycan.

The lycan stopped and went quiet for a moment seeming to just notice the open window. Persæus and Achilles had already raised their blades ready to do mortal damage that even lycan couldn't survive. It was just as though it had been written into a movie script when two of them stuck their heads out either side of the window. Persæus and Achilles swung with all their might decapitating two with hardly a whisper of a thud as the sharpened blades sliced cleanly through the beast's necks and their heads bounced off the garden soil below. Both men jumped down to the ground to wait out the third beast but it didn't appear. They wondered if they'd been premature in leaving the safety of their perch but they could hear the beast rummaging around in their room, they could only assume it was looking for something of value. Soon it went quiet and they felt like they should go around to the front and rear doors and see who, if anyone, was coming out the doors. Achilles went to the front and Persæus went to the rear after giving the blade back to Achilles. A handy tool up on the somewhat thin ledge, but he didn't really need it,

Soon, Persæus realized the malice they'd felt when they had walked into the pub as the bar maid walked out the back door. She smiled big at Persæus and said, "I'm going to have to eat that new server girl for dinner tonight, aren't I?"
Hearing voices Achilles ran around back just in time to see the two transform. Persæus was between him and the bar maid so he had to reposition himself to be of any use. The bar maid wasn't having it and rotated away from him howling loud and long.
"She's calling in reinforcements," growled Rover.
"There's more?" queried a shocked Achilles.
"You have no clue the can of worms you boys opened tonight," laughed the she wolf beast.
It wasn't long before they heard the pads and panting of three more beasts approaching. Upon hearing the clamor of her back up, she looked in their direction and in the moment, Achilles and Rover both jumped and destroyed her. She was the one that had opened a can of worms.
Rover flew up into the darkness of the cool night air and as the beasts spied Achilles, they charged in. Rover swooped in behind taking out two, one with each clawed hand around their necks; he landed with feet on their torsos and ripped their heads backward from their shoulders. The third met the lightning-fast

blades of Achilles and was decimated like a hog to the slaughter.

"Nice move, Rover."

"Thanks cousin."

Rover had never called Achilles cousin before and he was thinking it felt pretty good. It had a taken time, but Achilles had become accustomed to having conversations with both of Persæus alter egos.

They were both covered in blood and they wouldn't get out of town without raising alarms in that condition. Rover cupped his claws for Achilles to step up and lifted him into the window then jumped up after him. He shrank down to Persæus again and the two cleaned up. Zeus was already on body cleanup detail and a good thing too. The ruckus had not gone unnoticed and about the time the boys were done cleaning themselves off the police were sticking their heads in the door to find out what had happened. It took three hours to convince the police that two thugs had broken in to rob them and when they saw how big Persæus was and Achilles having two knives, they didn't want any part of them. The sun was already lighting the eastern horizon when they finally got the Lieutenant to call off the dogs. Getting any sleep at all was most certainly out of the question. There was nothing to do but walk to the train and sleep on the ride home. At least they had finished a day earlier than expected. Achilles was already asleep when Persæus thought to ask,

"Hey, Zeus? Question."

"Yes, son."

"What do you do with the mess we make?"

"I feed them to my pet sharks in the Mediterranean."

"Oh... I see... Remind me not to get on your bad side?"

"Too late for that, son. Way too late for that."

"Wonderful."

CHAPTER NINE: CHANGES OF THE HEART AND UNDERSHORTS

Getting home They determined to stop in at the shop and then head to their respective homes for a nap before coming back to start the day. When they got there, Danaë gave them what wasn't bad news but not necessarily welcome. Regardless, it was news nobody liked hearing. Isis wanted to transfer to Alex' shop to be just a couple of hours closer to her family in Cairo. His shipping and receiving coordinator had put in her notice because she was getting married and moving to Italy. Isis wanted to take advantage of the opportunity to cut four hours round trip time out of her visits to her family. Not only her very appreciated skills but also her extreme beauty would be missed in the shop. She had proven herself extremely competent they all felt sure she was a good part of the reason the company had grown the way it had. They would be hard pressed to replace her. Persæus was especially unhappy as the news truly hurt him. He had thought things might work out differently for the two of them. She did have a line on her replacement which would ease things for Achilles and the rest and she recommended a friend of her friend, someone Danaë had already spoken with and she hoped that it would work out for them all.

No one could deny her the chance to make the move and in fact a few men of the shop and Danaë had already volunteered to help her pack up and get her things shipped out. It was a perfect opportunity for Isis and if they moved fast on the new hire, Isis could train the person she was recommending before her final day. Of course, she and Danaë were two steps ahead of the curve and the young lady would be in that day to interview for the job. Achilles called a quick meeting with the executive staff and let them handle it.

"Persæus and I really need to get some sleep after the night we had, just figure it out for yourselves. We have to trust each other in these decisions."

Danaë spoke up, "She's hired! Well, as soon as the rest of you sign off. I spoke with her at length over the phone and I think she'll do quite nicely from what I can tell. But y'all get your say in the matter too. That's just my two cents."

"And your opinion counts for a lot," said Leon. He knew on which side his bread was buttered.

"She's been a shipping and receiving coordinator for another company in the past so, she's familiar with most of the processes we use. It's just the little nuances that would be different so, she should be able to slide right in, hit the floor running, as they say," said Isis.

"Okay, well, Persæus and I will introduce ourselves when we get back. Thanks everyone, see you this afternoon."

Achilles was pretty much just going through the motions as he was dead on his feet and he knew that Persæus couldn't be feeling too much different. The little bit of sleep they'd gotten on the train helped but they both needed to get a few more hours. They said goodbye at the usual intersection and walked to their respective homes, they both crashed on their respective couches in their respective living rooms irrespective of each other. And they slept.

Hunger wakened Achilles and drew him from the pleasant

dreams of beautiful women and brave men that sometimes graced his sleep. Living as long as he had, he had seen so many, that no face seemed brand new to him anymore and so his dreams were not about anyone and still about everyone he'd ever known. It was surreal at times living among the humans for so long, but having Persæus and his Auntie Danaë this close at hand for the past several years had been a real blessing. It was almost like being back at Mount Olympus among the gods, except that he had to make his own meals, wash his own dishes, fold his own clothes and work for his living... Well, maybe not so much like being back on Olympus but he did praise Zeus for saving him and giving him a second chance in this world, regardless.

He made himself a lamb, lettuce and tomato sandwich on wheat bread slathered with cucumber sauce. It just didn't get any better than this. Life among the humans had so many perks including many of the delicacies. Regardless of his musings and considerations of this world he wondered if Zeus would ever invite him back among the gods? Never the less it was good to be on his good side and be able to spend so much time with his cousin and auntie. He locked up his house and headed into work, curious what this new person would be like that Auntie Danaë liked her so much.

Persæus wakened groggy and not quite ready to face what was left of the day. He so often spent more time at the shop than at home and so seldom took any extra days off, except to hunt of course, but even that had suffered at times. He was simply happy to have bottomed out the lycan issue, at least he hoped it was over. They had dealt a blow to Ba'al and his followers the sting of which they would feel for a long time to come and he was glad that Zeus had given them the task; now that it was through, anyway. He hadn't been too excited about it before they started it, but in all, it had turned out well. He wasn't feeling hungry when he rose but on the walk into work, he grabbed some street food as the ache in his stomach made itself apparent. He was looking forward to meeting this new person they were probably going to hire to replace Isis. He was thinking probably, because his mother's word tended to carry a lot of weight with Achilles and the rest. She was well liked and even more well respected.

Persæus walked in just after Achilles by only a few minutes and noticed there was a strange buzz about the shop, nothing defined but it was as though something great was happening. He saw his mother and asked, "Did we get a new contract or something?"

She told him, "Why don't you go talk with Achilles, he'll fill you in."

The broad knowing smile on her face made him pause to think there had to be something up that was going make him extraordinarily happy or kick him in the eggs; would that make his mother smile? He hoped it wasn't the eggs. He saw Achilles back by the vault and walked over to say hello.

"Hey, cousin," said Achilles. "I thought you'd abandoned us. Nice of you to show up."

"Why? When did you come in?"

"About ten minutes ago."

"Of course."

"Walk with me, talk with me," said Achilles.

"Your momma is manipulating and conniving, in a good way, of course. I think she has plans for you and Andromeda."

"Who's Andromeda?"

"She's our new shipping and receiving coordinator. Don't even argue, you don't get a choice in the matter in spite of what you were told. The others made the decision just like I'd asked them. I hate it when that happens," he quipped.

As the two men walked back to shipping and receiving. Persæus looked back over his shoulder at his mother as she smiled like the Cheshire Cat and then turned away to whatever it was she had been doing.

They reached the warehouse where shipping and Receiving was

situated and Persæus didn't see anyone immediately. Both Isis and Andromeda were in the office busy going over paperwork when the boys walked in.

"Andy, I'd like you to meet my cousin and Danaë's son; this is Persæus."

Persæus was dumfounded and couldn't speak, couldn't think and was barely able to put out his hand to shake that of Andromeda. His mouth agape, Achilles raised his hand and closed it for him. The girls laughed. Isis was most certainly one of the most beautiful women in the entire world but Andromeda, she was above and beyond spectacular by a kilometer, at least. Her infectious and endearing smile couldn't be avoided or denied, it made Persæus feel like a pubescent boy with butterflies in his stomach.

"Very pleased to meet you," she said.

"I assure you; the pleasure is all mine, Andromeda."

"Please call me Andy, it's so much easier to say and spell."

Andromeda smiled with a tiny curtsy as she said this, her blonde hair bouncing as she did so. She was wearing red tennis shoes which was surprising but it said she had come in ready to work. She was a bit under two meters tall standing just at Persæus' chin and weighed hardly an ounce. Also surprising was the white cotton dress with printed large dark red roses with green thornless stems and leaves; the petals to match those red tennis shoes. A loosely cinched red cloth belt that accentuated her microscopic waist and ample breasts. Dressed to impress was an understatement. Isis just smiled and tried not to laugh as Persæus obviously couldn't get enough of Andy the eye candy.

"Have you found a place to live?" inquired Persæus.

"I'm in a little extended stay hotel just up the road from here but I've put in my application for Isis' place and she's put in a good word for me. If they give it to me, I'll just move in when she's done moving out. Would you happen to be interested in helping me move, boss?" She cocked her head a bit to the side moving her silken hair about her face as she spoke, twisting on her feet to make her dress float about her. This girl did not miss a beat in casting her hook.

"If we have the time free from work, I'd be happy to help out," Persæus took the bait willingly and almost gleefully.

Achilles thought it might be time to break up this moment of too obvious mutual admiration, "Cousin, what do you say we get some work done today. Bad enough we didn't get in here until noon today."

Persæus, still looking at Andy said, "It's tough to be the boss," he smiled and turned away to exit the door.

"So glad to meet you, boss," said Andy.

Persæus turned back, "Very happy to have you onboard."

The boys left the room and as the door closed the girls burst into laughter as the attraction had been so extremely obvious; it embarrassed Persæus to no end especially as he thought so highly of Isis; but he couldn't help himself. He and Achilles laughed as well when they had gotten far enough away.

Achilles elbowed Persæus, "Your future ex?"

"Let's hope it works out far better than that!"

"I think I mentioned on the way over here, I suspect your mom and Isis had this planned at some point."

"Oh, ya think?"

"Just maybe… Pretty much sure of it… Ya."

Angel put in his two cents, "Fools rush in where Angel fears to tread."

"Thanks, good buddy," said Persæus.

Not wanting to be outdone, Rover mentioned, "She looks delicious!"

"Whoa boy, slow down."

"Right; tasty?"

"Oh, that's supposed to be better?"

"A little, maybe?"

The four of them laughed together and it was a cacophony.

Danaë was busily working away with a giant smile on her face.

Isis' last two weeks with them flew by all too fast and they were heartbroken to see her go even though she was still technically with the company. But a company sendoff party was in order and they had a catered event such that there were plenty of left overs the employees could take home to their families to enjoy. They just needed to supply their own takeaway boxes; the caterer didn't supply those as it wasn't common an employer would spend extra like this. The spread was absolutely scrumpdillyishous and it covered the better part of two eight-foot tables with hot and cold dishes, green salad, fruit salad, slider burgers, fish, lamb, spaghetti, mac and cheese and a myriad of desserts; Persæus favorite part of the meal.

Andy didn't over do things at work but she did her share today of monopolizing Persæus' time and he didn't mind. Funny thing, neither did his mother or Achilles as they had with Isis; Persæus had not figured that one out yet. Maybe it was the difference in their vertical attributes. Maybe it was because she was Persian and prone to Islam; he didn't think of it until now but the Battle of Thermopylæ could explain that. Prejudices from that battle could very well run deep in some people. He didn't know and he didn't really care, he wanted their approval on whomever he chose so he respected their wishes. It seemed this was their wish and she really was right up his alley. It was a Friday so they could close the loading doors early and the men that had volunteered were able to go with Isis to help her load her apartment into a cargo truck. Persæus and another group of men were all going to continue to work to clean up the schedule and then would help Andy move into the same apartment on Saturday.

Saturday morning at eight o'clock they all met at Andy's extended stay, including Achilles, Danaë and some of the guys from the shop. They found that Andy had already packed most everything, she was on top of the situation and ready to make it happen. Of course, the big stuff she had was just stacked into a corner because the extended stay was already furnished but her preparedness was impressive. She was dressed to impress again as well. Her hair pulled back into a pony tail through a red ball cap, dressed in her black spandex pants and a well fit white cotton button up collared shirt straight out of a women's Business Magazine. This girl had every bit as much style as Isis or his mother. With as much help as they had, it didn't take long to load the truck and roll on over to Isis' old place and now Andy's new place. There was maybe a kilometer or so in between the two with the shop midway between as well, making it an easy walk to get into work from her new location as well. It was working well for Andy and it almost seemed there was more than just these three women in this little plan. On the drive over, Persæus was in the back of the tuck so he called out to Zeus.

"Zeus?" He inquired. And there was no answer… His father seldom ignored him and this stunk as though Zeus had been caught in one of his far to common meddling's for which he was well known.

"Father, I'm not taking no for an answer."

"Oh, bother! What is it this time, Persæus?"

"You know what it is father."

"All right, yes! Are you happy now that you know?"

"I'm not happy about that. I'm happy that you both think highly enough of her that you have brought her to me."

"Persæus, we both know that you are an intelligent person and can choose for yourself, BUT, and it's a big but, no, hers is tiny, the but I'm talking about is this: Sometimes parents feel their children need a nudge in not necessarily the right direction, we can't always know what will be right, but maybe call it a better direction."

"I could tell that mother and Achilles were keeping Isis and myself apart. Why is that?"

"Isis is a plenty good person and I'm sure you two would have been happy. But her family is from Egypt and we need you here to help your cousin and we wanted to see you keeping the family close at hand. Chances are, and I think that is obvious now, she would eventually have wanted to move back to Egypt. Even with being omniscient I can't say for certain as timelines change for the sake of that Christian free will thing, but my vision suggested that would happen sooner or later."

"Okay, I can't say I appreciate the interference but at least now I understand and I appreciate you talking with me. I certainly can't complain about whom you have put in front of me, that's a real true fact. She is incredible!"

"We're glad you think so. I hope you will always think so, you will have centuries together if you so choose."

"I'm ready to look at the possibility. It seems I've been single far too long and I'd like to find out if this is the real thing."

"Well, I'm glad you are pleased and I think you will find Andromeda to be everything you have ever hoped for, and maybe then some. Take your time, you have forever so you don't need to rush in where Angel fears to tread. Yes, I was listening. I thought he was rather humorous."

"Thanks, Zeus!" said Angel.

"And then what Rover said?" inquired Persæus.

"Yes, keep him on a leash."

"I heard that," said Rover.

"I know. You were meant to hear it. Sit, boy, sit."

"Okay, ha, ha. I'll find a way to get back at you for that one, old man."

"Careful with the old man stuff, I'll give you arthritis."

"Ouch!"

"Thanks for talking with me father."

"You're welcome son. Give it time and you will likely see the wisdom in what has happened."

They had arrived at Isis' old place and it seemed almost a betrayal to move another woman into it. But oh, what a woman! He already missed seeing Isis' smiling face among the familiar furniture and wall hangings as he walked in the door and his heart ached as he realized he was going to miss her more than he thought possible and would likely need some time to adjust to the new situation. He couldn't move right on from considering

Isis and just latch onto Andy; as tempting as that was. Even a demi god had emotions that needed to be settled. His talk with Zeus had given him a new perspective on the situation and he was ready to look at it more objectively; especially as Isis had been involved in the decision. That meant she had seen issues about which she had spoken to Danaë and not spoken to him; that hurt just a bit, but that was then and this would likely be his future, he thought. He understood there was wisdom in having his mother and father involved in such decisions even at his age. Isis would forever be a truly special part of his life and he needed to get that chapter compartmentalized before moving on.

Andy was there taking charge, not only moving boxes and unpacking but gently instructing everyone as to where everything must go and how it should be arranged. Persæus had never seen his mother take such a back seat to a younger woman but she simply followed instructions and helped wherever she could. He knew in his heart of hearts that his parents and even Isis had made a good decision in bringing in Andy to help build the company and become a part of his life; part of all their lives. They had the truck unloaded in almost no time with so many actors participating and soon the men took the truck back to the shop and took the rest of the day off. Persæus, Achilles and Danaë stayed for a couple of more hours helping Andy unpack and turn the place into something of her own.

As Andy put her own belongings around the place, her pictures, paintings, photos and furniture, it slowly lost the memories of Isis that still lingered. They would not be gone completely for some time but as it filled with a new woman, the previous one, although still present, was fading, ever so slowly. Danaë could read Persæus face and knew the agony he was experiencing. She could tell it had not become real for him until just this moment and she knew it was tearing him apart. It would take time and it would be a good change, but he would have to suffer through the emotional turmoil of a change he had not expected. So many would not expect a man to experience the emotional pain of changing an entire expected path in life. But women don't usually understand the turmoil a man experiences when the rug is pulled out from under him. Even when it is replaced with one that is likely of better quality for his eventual realization. That isn't because men are hard of heart or unfeeling, but rather because men are taught from a young age to never let emotion rule them publicly, regardless of the fact that it does, privately. He was elated and devastated at the same time; it was the most heart wrenching of possibilities he had ever experienced. At the same time, he wanted to soar on the wings of Rover and die by the hands of Angel. It would take time.

Achilles had ordered pizza and ale while they worked and after a break for lunch, they were able to finally break down the last of the boxes that had held Andy's belongings. She was elated it had gone so well and so quickly and her glee was infectious. They all felt good simply in response to her joy; Persæus had never met anyone that could bring that kind of delight to a room. She was a breath of fresh air, a spring breeze and a field of flowers; it was as though she exuded happiness form every pour. Even though it was obvious Danaë had loved Isis, she was a different and more joyous person around Andy. Persæus wondered if that was just the newness of the relationship or if that would last. The job was done but the three stuck around for a bit to finish off a couple more ales. It was a nice time of bonding and it felt like Andy would fit right in.

The weekend always went by too quickly as it usually did for Achilles, being a confirmed bachelor, he seldom did much but watch football during the season or fish in one of the many streams that were nearby. Work had pervaded every part of his life to this point but now the company was stable and had good people to operate it when he wanted time off. The challenges of the recent quest and the events leading up to it had left him thinking it was time to take a break from the rigors of daily life. But that was not going to happen as Zeus didn't have any plans for him but someone else did. Ba'al that had devised new mischief by planting the seeds of suspicion in the mind of the Corporate Tax Administration which now wanted access to Achilles vault. Achilles sauntered into work Monday morning thinking it would be just another day, but waiting by the man door entry was a stranger in a suit.

"Hello, I'm John Thedopolis from the Corporate Tax Administration, I'm hoping you have a few minutes to talk this morning."

"Nice to meet you, how may I help?"

"Why don't we go inside, you may want to have your tax preparer join us."

"Why is that?"

"I've found what appear to be discrepancies in some of your documentation and I'd like to check it over with whomever is your preparer."

"I take care of everything to do with the taxes, you can ask me."

"Shall we go in?"

"We shall not, not until you specify the discrepancies you would like to discuss."

"It would be much easier inside where we can sit and look at your papers."

"I'd be happy to accommodate you, Mr. Thedopolis but you'll need to call and make an appointment. I have more than my share of things to do today."

"We can do this the easy way or the hard way. It's your choice."

Persæus, coming into work, had just walked up behind Mr. Thedopolis.

"I've offered you the easy way, Mr. Thedopolis, I am hoping you don't want to find out what the truly hard way is. Hey, Persæus. This is Mr. Thedopolis from the Corporate Tax Administration. He was waiting for me this morning and wants to take a look at our books. I've asked him to call and make an appointment but he's threatening me."

Persæus stepped up a foot closer to John Thedopolis as he turned to look, so that Thedopolis had to crane his neck to look up at him and he let Rover answer. In his deepest and most menacing voice he said, "So good to make your acquaintance Mr. Thedopolis; how old are you?"

"I'm not accustomed to answering personal questions, why do you want to know?"

"Because, if you want to be another year older, you'll call and make the appointment," his eyes glowing red…

Achilles about busted a gut. He knew Persæus would be assertive but he didn't expect him to unleash the dog.

Mr. Thedopolis very curtly and fair running yelled, "I'll be calling you."

"Probably a good idea," Angel yelled after him as he moved swiftly away.

"Not a bad way to start the day," said Angel to Achilles.

"I can think of better ways but it was kind of fun," said Achilles.

"He was just waiting for you?" asked Persæus.

"Ya, a bit odd. I thought they always sent a letter or something."

"That's the way I've always heard it was done."

"Something smells off to me."

"When he calls make sure the call goes to you and ask him for his supervisor's phone number before talking to him."

Achilles opened the door and shut off the alarm, opened the roll up door to let the light in.

"I suppose I should have a tax accountant doing the work but importing spread sheets into our tax application is a no brainer. And it's a salary I don't have to pay."

"Good thing, you can pay my exorbitant salary that way," laughed Persæus.

"Right?"

It wasn't long before John Thedopolis called and asked to make an appointment to see Achilles and his accountant. Danaë sent it through to Achilles and he was already loaded for bear.

"Mr. Thedopolis or should I say John? Oh, really? You'd rather I call you Mr. Thedopolis? Well, John, it's like this. I need to speak with your supervisor. You see, the usual route is for the tax office to send me a letter and ask me to call them. That makes me wonder if you are on the straight and narrow. You're on the straight and narrow aren't you, John? What's your supervisor's name and phone number, John? What do you mean you don't need to give me that? Of course you do! Now, what is that again? John? John? Are you there, John? Hmmm, must have lost the connection."

Standing nearby, Danaë commented, "Even one sided, that was an interesting call."

"Yes, I hope that is the end of the interest, I just don't need this today or any day," his frustration being obvious.

Achilles assumed that was the end of the tax questions but was just as sure, John could be calling again. It seemed likely either way depending on what John's true intentions were. There had been nothing that should have alerted the Tax Administration to anything. He filed and paid his taxes on time all the time. He wondered if there was something more to John's curiosity and was hoping this morning's shenanigans were not the instrument of some other force being used against him and/or the company. If the man came back again without hearing from his supervisor, Achilles would be dealing more harshly with the situation. He told Persæus about the phone call to gain his input and he agreed, it just wasn't right and it would be wise to try and get to the bottom of the situation. They coordinated to arrive at about the same time every morning just in case Thedopolis tried another surprise appearance.

About three in the afternoon, a couple of police officers stopped by to speak with Achilles; He didn't like that at all.

"Are you Mr. Achilles Olympus?"

"Yes, how may I help you?"

"We have a warrant for your arrest. Would you please put your hands behind your back."

"No. I'd like to see the warrant."

"We won't ask you nicely a second time Mr. Olympus."

"I don't care whether you do or not. May I Please see the Warrant?"

"Just do as we ask," the officer radioed for back up.

About that time Persæus had walked over and one of the officers covered his weapon with his hand, "Back up sir, back up!"

"Mr. Olympus asked you very nicely to show him the warrant you claim you have. Mr. Olympus is very nice, me; I'm not so Nice. Show him the warrant!"

"Sir! Back off or we will have to arrest you too!"

"Good luck with that!" said Persæus as he allowed Angel to grow him to his full height.

The officers were amazed and aghast at the little magic trick Persæus performed and they drew and aimed their weapons.

"Officers, that is a mistake you don't want to make, I suggest you holster your weapons and chill your sh!t'" said Rover as Persæus eyes began to glow. They began to back up one slow step at a time and rover started growing his ears and fangs. He was having fun toying with the officers as one began to piss himself. He knew they would never be believed if they said anything to anyone outside of the shop. About that time more squad cars were arriving and driving right in through the open warehouse door. The men in both shops and shipping and receiving, put down their work and moved toward the commotion as others closed down the drive through doors in the other two shops. They did not appreciate the invasion into their realm and they would defend their friend and employer as they knew better than to allow the authorities to overstep their limits. Something other people around the world seemed to have forgotten was to stand firm in their integrity; they had not been raised to believe in themselves or their God given rights as human beings as had the men of Achilles.

Persæus turned to the officers hiding behind their car doors and laughed as they sunk down in fear as though he would shoot bullets from his glowing eyes. At this point his wings began to unfurl and he let out an ear shattering howl and proclaimed, "In the name of Zeus, I command you to put down your weapons and cease your hostilities or this will end in our own demise! Do as you are commanded and live!"

He allowed his clawed hands to form and his fur to grow out such that he took on the full form of Rover. With the full size of Angel, which he had never allowed in the past, at nearly four meters in height he was truly an awe full spectacle to behold. The officers opened fire out of fear as Rover had done nothing aggressive but command their obedience. He folded his wings around himself and steeled his feathers as an impenetrable shield around him standing fearless and immortal in his greatest form of all three beings in one. He was, invincible. The bullets that had penetrated him prior to encompassing his wings around himself were pushed from his skin and dropped to the floor below his wings and he laughed long and loud such that everyone knew he was in charge, alive and well.

The officers reloaded their weapons and continued to fire running themselves out of ammunition. They were now very afraid and they knew it was a lost cause but they had never been trained for utter defeat. They called in their national Special Suppressive Antiterrorist Unit (EKAM) and the city's Special Missions Department (TEIDA). There was no EKAM unit in Phthia so it would take some time for a unit to arrive but the locals knew the TEIDA would be arriving in short order and they hid behind their squad cars. The men of the shop still holding their tools in their hands now knowing the officers were without ammunition rushed in beating the officers and the squad cars mercilessly. As they did so, Rover uncovered himself and started grabbing the squad cars and tossing them out the door in a pile in the street such that no other vehicles could pass. He created a blockade of immense proportion and the officers ran scared out of their minds out the door and dispersed down the streets running for their very lives. A roar of victory went up from the men and they gathered about Rover. None of the officers had been mortally wounded and those with minor injuries were led to the door and unceremoniously tossed into the street like drunks bounced out of a pub.

The TEIDA arrived and the tactical officers pouring into the street looked around dumbfounded. They could only wonder at the retreating patrolmen and look at each other as they observed the mangled cars and the last few bloodied officers picking themselves up after being bounced out of the warehouse. Seeing their confusion, Rover roared in earth shattering volume and howled to the heavens bringing pain to those that didn't cover their ears. Many of the TEIDA hilariously scrambled to get back into their vehicles pissing themselves and cowering inside in fear as they had never experienced true hostility from an immortal enemy. The remaining tactical officers hid behind the barricade of vehicles piled up in the street, not knowing what to do and not listening to their commanding officer that was telling them to charge in. Nope, nada, that wasn't going to happen and they let him know in no uncertain terms even telling him to go in if he was so brave. The response was very nearly comical and anyone watching from afar had to be laughing at the lunacy of the situation.

Achilles knew this was an absolute cluster and called up to Rover for a little conference. Angel shrank Rover down to mortal size and simply said, "What's up Cus?"
"I think our men are in danger and I'm not sure we should continue this course."
"What do you propose we do, invite them in for tea?"
"Well, not exactly but…" he spoke quietly to Rover and then told the men to get back against the walls away from the open door. Achilles and Rover walked up to the door dead centered with Rover standing behind Achilles.
"Those men arrived and tried to arrest me without a warrant. We asked to see the warrant they claimed to have. They

refused to produce a warrant. You men can see here what has happened before your arrival, do you really want to see what can happen if you don't leave?" With that, Rover spread his wings and looked back and forth at the men still standing but also shaking in their boots. "I'll give you the same choice we had given the others before they got stupid and fired on us, we were not the aggressors!! Leave now or die!" None of the men previously had died but Achilles had to give them fair warning that it was a possibility. He and Rover could see them talking among themselves and many were nodding as though they were approving what Achilles had said.

It seemed almost forever that nothing happened It was obviously pandemonium amongst the aggressors and they had no clue what to do as they waited for their commander to respond. Finally, someone with eggs approached, slowly, warily, keeping a hand on his service weapon and an eye on rover.

"You're Achilles Olympus?" Asked the player.

"Yes, who's asking?"

"I am commander Thedopolis:

"Thedopolis, as in tax man Thedopolis?"

"If you are speaking of John Thedopolis, then yes. He's my brother."

"Have you spoken with him today?"

"Yes, he says you refused to show him your books and got aggressive with him. Then things escalated to this point. Why didn't you just show him your books?"

"Why should I?"

"Because he asked nicely."

"And I refused… Nicely."

"I don't think you realize how much trouble you're in right now."

"I don't think you realize that I'm not the one in trouble."

Rover growled a low menacing growl that rumbled right to commander Thedopolis' heart. "I consider that a threat to my life and right now I can arrest you both."

Rover laughed, "They tried that already, would you care to go for

O-shit and Two?"

"Look, EKAM will be here soon and then it's out of my hands, I won't be able to help you. If you let me arrest you and take you in, the situation becomes moot and EKAM goes away."

"Oh, you think you are offering me a deal I can't refuse?"

"It's better than the alternative."

"Let me clue you in on the alternative… Rover, blow him away."

With that the commander went for his weapon, but he could barely unholster it before Rover started flapping his wings and growing in size. The wind beneath his wings hit the commander like a ton of bricks and he was thrown backward and as Rover grew, the commander just kept flying through the air. It was hilarious and the men along the walls of the shop were laughing and slapping each other on the back as Rover kept the commander flying.

No one had any intention of backing down as commander Thedopolis being just as stupid or influenced by Ba'al as had been his brother, was just too stubborn to know when he'd been properly beaten. Rover and Achilles walked back into the shop and they closed the roll up door as the squad cars were no longer an issue.

"I'd tell you men to go home for the day but I'm afraid they might try to arrest you for some phony reason. If you'd like, you can stay or take your chances with the morons outside."

Everyone gathered around Achilles and Rover and voiced their unwavering support and desire to stay and help them in this fight. It was just as heart touching as it was stupid but no one saw that they had another choice. They were in it to win it and nothing could deter them from the unmistakable end of the story. In their minds, one did not pick up their toys and run home to mommy just because the other kid had called in his big brother.

If and when EKAM arrived, they would deal with the consequences. Achilles told the men that should EKAM show up, and they very likely would, they were to assume their positions along the wall but stay hidden, they were not to reveal they were there and possibly it would be assumed they had somehow snuck out. They would open the doors and provide Rover as a target again hoping to run out their ammunition, again. They didn't really expect that to work twice but it worked well the first time, it was worth trying to at least reduce the ammunition count before a full-on confrontation. The biggest worry was that the TEIDA was bringing in more ammunition and that they'd be dealing with double fudge the second time around. Of course, that second concern only applied to the officers that hadn't pissed their pants and were still hanging around. Even in the short time that Commander Thedopolis had been talking it had been observed that several of the TEIDA force had walked away behind the commander's back.

Then Leon and Joseph came rolling in with four by eight-foot sheets of six-millimeter-thick steel from the receiving area. Leon said, "Andy said you'd be grateful for this. We already put it up in the receiving area and clamped it to the roll up door. We can have it done here in ten minutes as well. Then we'll get it done in the small parts area. She's a genius! We moved stacks of other supplies in behind it to keep it from being disturbed and we can put machines behind it in here and in small parts. Come on guys, lend a hand!"

Persæus and Achilles had to admit it was a great idea if they could keep the TEIDA forces from dozing the barricade away. They didn't think there was much of a chance of that unless the locals had been granted the rights to bring in an actual bull dozer. And TEIDA couldn't anticipate this move on the part of those inside unless they had someone on the inside themselves, which at this point, they had to assume they did not.

"Danaë!" Called Achilles, "Why does the phone keep ringing?"
"ERT (Ellinikí RadioPhonía Tileórasi) from Athens wants to know what's going on!"

"Seriously? They've already heard of this?"

"I've been sending them video and they want to talk with you… you and the talking monster."

"Oh, great! They know about our talking monster! Have you been sending them video of Rover as well?"

"No, nephew, I'm not stupid. That must be from other reports."

"I know you're not stupid Auntie, I had to ask to know what's going on."

"All right, you're forgiven… this time."

"Record me, Auntie. I'll give them an earful."

"Ah, ah, ah! Record me Danaë," said Andy. "I'm prettier and they'll believe a pretty face before Achilles ugly mug."

"Hey, now! Right or not, be nice!"

"Of course, boss. But you know I'm right. Pretty is good, Disney Studios proved that."

"It's all yours, ladies."

"John Thedopolis, with the Corporate Tax Administration tried to violate the rights of a local business man by trespassing and forcing Mr. Achilles Olympus of A & N The Works Fabrications, into providing his tax records without cause. When Mr. Olympus refused and chased the rogue agent off the property, Mr. Thedopolis incorporated two local police officers, claiming to have a warrant for Mr. Olympus arrest, they tried to arrest Mr. Olympus but refused to produce said warrant upon request. They also were chased from the property. The area police were chased away by men with work tools as well, after they had fired upon Mr. Olympus without provocation. The area TEIDA are now on location, led by Commander Thedopolis, brother of the rogue agent who has threatened death upon Mr. Olympus when the EKAM from Athens arrive. Nothing like a little family affair to spell corruption. Reporting live for ERT Athens from Phthia Greece, this is Andromeda Æthiopia."

It wasn't long after that they heard the sound of a helicopter over the area but they weren't sure if it was the police or ERT

Athens. The phone slowed just a bit but Danaë reported there were other news stations clamoring for the video that she had given to ERT. ERT didn't have exclusive rights to the videos so she figured, why not? She gave them everything and Andy's face was all over Greece and a great deal of all of Europe. Danaë kept a small TV in her office and she had been watching it most of the day. Now she saw Andy's face come on and she called everyone around to watch it. Andy's synopsis along with her pretty face had captured anyone within a 1000 Kilometer radius and they would be blowing up the phone before the day was over. It turned out that ERT Athens had sent a chopper up to video the overhead of the situation. That was very good for the people inside The Works because they could see the TEIDA setting what looked like explosives around all the shops to blow out the walls.

"Zeus! This is too much for us to handle, can you get the explosives?"

"Consider it done! Hey, that commander Thedopolis, did he look like he might have heart problems?" and Zeus was gone again; although, so was commander Thedopolis. They life flighted him out with the ERT chopper. They would find out later that Commander Thedopolis did not have the authority to use explosives under the circumstances. By taking him out of the equation, Zeus had effectively punished the guilty party and no one else wanted to subvert the chain of command and use what had not been authorized. EKAM finally arrived but they were not as gung-ho as TEIDA had been. They were willing to wait. After assessing the situation, a single man approached the man door and knocked; gently.

"We Understand there may have been a little confusion," said the EKAM commander, "I'm captain Horacio. My I speak to whomever is in charge?"

"I'm Achilles Olympus, how may I help you?"

"That's quite some news caster you've got there. Both the president and the prime minister have been on the phone with my boss. We've been instructed to investigate this before doing something we might all regret."

"We would certainly appreciate that."

"Would you be willing to come out and speak with me?"

"No, but you can come in and speak with me."

"I told them that's what you would say, but nobody listens to me. That's fine, I'll come in, may I use your lavatory?"

"Certainly."

"Show me where to go? Thanks. Is it true what this Andromeda reported?"

"We've got more than forty men and a half dozen department heads that will swear to it."

"I kind of figured that. If that's true, it will take a bit of time to unravel this mess but I think you folks can relax."

"Well, thank you for that but I think we will stay wound up until it is unraveled, if you don't mind."

"I don't mind, just don't let the dogs out, if you know what I mean," as Captain Horacio winked at Achilles.

Achilles was suspicious then but not in a bad way. When Captain Horacio was done in the lavatory, he came out wiping his freshly washed hands so Achilles knew his need wasn't any type of ruse. "You see, we've been getting reports of disturbances all over Greece with Phthia being at the center of the issues. Somehow, you and a giant man named Persæus keep seeping into the conversation and people are talking of a large wolflike creature. Now the rub, arbitrary murders have stopped where these two have been seen. We can't be more grateful but it sure would be nice to have an explanation and there are rumors about what has happened here today. Could you maybe enlighten me?"

"You seem like a reasonable man and as much as I'd like to accommodate you, the answer is, no. But you also seem very intelligent and I don't want to insult your intelligence so, let's just say, we're on the same side and I would like to promote a little mutual respect. You're a smart man captain, you can figure it out."

"I see. Not exactly the answer for which I was looking. Still, I have to consider what I'd do if the situation was reversed. I'm going to go out here and do a little of that investigation stuff my boss wants done. Promise you folks won't cause any trouble?"

"We certainly won't initiate it; we might finish it though. Do me one favor?"

"That all depends."

"Commander Thedopolis planted explosives around the building..."

"What!"

"I assure you it's true. We saw it being done, live from the ERT chopper. Could you have those removed?"

"If that is the case, I'll get them removed and then have Thedopolis removed from the force, permanently."

"Thank you, Captain."

"By the way, you can get the footage from ERT of the explosives being set. I swear to you, they showed it being done on live TV!"

"By the gods! Thank you, Mr. Olympus"

The two men shook hands and the captain left.

Hours passed and everyone was getting hungry and tired. Many had found a place on the floor to rest and Danaë and Andy were both sitting in the office with their heads laying on the desk. The evening came and went and nighttime began to congeal, daylight giving way to the darkness and the moon rising to light a traveler's way. Finally, captain Horacio was knocking on the door again and Achilles yelled across the shop for someone to let him in. He just about ran across to meet him as he came in smiling just a whisp of a smile. It appeared to Achilles that Captain Horacio had confirmed their story and he was anxious to know the verdict. That was indeed as it happened to be and all in the shop were happy that someone finally believed what had actually occurred. Much of the reason Captain Horacio could clear their good names hinged on the videos Danaë had live streamed to ERT. Everything checked out except the ludicrous claims of a giant wolf with wings that tried to eat everyone. Captain tried again to get information on that little tidbit but lips were tight and all he got for his trouble was knowing smiles. He suspected there was far more to it than he might ever know.

At that moment Persæus asked Zeus to do a little mind erasure except for that of Captain Horacio; he felt they might need his cooperation in the future and Zeus agreed. Looking into his mind Zeus found a particularly good and true spirit that he liked and he let Captain Horacio continue to wonder about the giant winged wolf; but only as a haunting recurring dream that entertained his thoughts in that place between wakefulness and sleep. And then there was the matter of the mangled squad cars and that of course was a snap to clean up. The fleet managers were going to have a heck of a time reconciling that little debacle but nobody cared. Let them wonder what happened, it's the officers that were trying to kill Rover that would have to explain the loss of the vehicles and that was not going to worry anyone at A & N The Works.

What to do about John Thedopolis of the Corporate Tax administration… That was a tough one because it had to be something that would deter him from ever again pulling such a stunt. It really wasn't a real lesson but they decided to give him explosive diarrhea for a week with a case of allergies to cause him to sneeze. In many ways it was a perfect punishment for such a shitty person. They also let him remember everything, every detail of every moment such that he would eventually be diagnosed with Maladaptive Daydreaming with possible Ecstasy and Lycanthropy. He would be locked in a mental institution for the rest of his life on drugs with names no one could pronounce. Zeus could be really creative when he wanted and everyone encouraged his onery streak in this particular case. There wasn't much anyone could do about Ba'al setting this scenario adrift in their lives but Andy suggested the perfect gift and Zeus sent him a paint and glitter bomb. He could clean it up with a snap of his fingers but it would be enough to let him know they had gotten the better of him. Zeus allowed them to watch Ba'al open it and for him to hear them all laughing, that was probably the very best part of it.

The next day they had to pull down all the barricades and restock the materials. They epoxied patches and painted all the bullet holes around the shop that had ricochet off of rover's wings. It was a bit of a mess, but everyone worked to get it done and it only took the better part of one day. They had lost time on the weekly schedule but ERT Athens was a station that most people in the area watched and it wasn't hard to call their customers and let them know they would do their best to catch up. The worst part was that everyone wanted to know all the tiniest details. The ladies had their hands full trying to get through the entire list of orders that would be affected but they managed to do so with every bit of grace one might hope to have in that situation. Danaë and Andy were truly godsends and they made the place run like clockwork.

Andy asked Danaë, "Is this how things always are around here?"
"Well, not always. Just most of the time. Not really, we have had our share of adventures but we seem to get through them well enough."
"I think I like it!"
"You, young lady, will fit right in!"
"When is that baby girl due to make an appearance?"
"It will be another two months; I'm getting to the really uncomfortable stage and I have to pee all the time!"
"Do you think she might be like Persæus?"
"I asked Zeus and he only says, "I'll never tell," like he's keeping some big secret."
"Well, that's got to be frustrating!"
"He can be terrible at times but it's just his sense of humor and he knows I'll love her regardless. I can live with it."
"You are much more patient than I could ever be."
"I doubt that, I see how you deal with these men around here."
"It's easy when my heart is set on one."

"I'm glad to know that. Just be patient with him, he has had a lot to get through and get over. I have no doubt he'll come around."

"I know he will also, Zeus guaranteed it."

"Did he now? I'll have to have a talk with that man."

Zeus interjected, "Don't worry dear, I'm not meddling. I simply looked ahead and it's going to work out just fine."

"All right, if that's all you did."

"I assure you both, Andy will have his full attention before long."

They both looked at each other and giggled, they knew this was a great family they had among the humans and it would last for many centuries, Zeus willing.

Achilles and Persæus sat down and looked over the finances to be sure they could afford it and decided to give all the men and the ladies a €500.00 bonus for the day. It wasn't much but they had shown extreme bravery and loyalty in the face of overwhelming danger. So many might have coward in the corners but these men and ladies, had gold running in their veins. It was the very least they could do for such integrity.

"Do you think we'll have more to deal with?" Persæus asked Achilles.

"It's hard to say, Set is no longer a problem but who knows about Ba'al? That was a truly incredible look on his face when the paint and glitter bomb went off!"

"I know! I wish we could do it again."

"Already a step ahead of you boys!"

"Right on, Zeus!" they both said at once.

The whole shop heard a poofing noise and several curse words from Ba'al. The laughter that broke out was infectious and with that, they heard more cursing from Ba'al.

"You know, Achilles. You were right when you told me so many years ago, this living among mortals isn't bad at all," proclaimed Persæus.

"I told you it would grow on you. Are you getting past Isis leaving?"

"That meant a whole lot more to me than I had thought. She was a very special lady and having her leave like that about ripped my heart out. I'm getting better, it's good to have Andy here as she is such a wonderful distraction."

"Well, I hope that she's more than JUST a distraction."

"Oh, yes; and so much more. I just need to take it slow and be sure I'm past all that's in the past. That was years of my life."

"That's a good plan. I say that because her parents are coming for a visit and she was a bit scared to mention it. She doesn't want you to feel like she's pushing you. It was their idea because they wanted to meet the people she's working with and where she is living."

"She hadn't mentioned it, I'm surprised."

"If you can imagine Andy being shy, she was concerned most of all about mentioning it to you. That's why I brought it up. It's just a visit and she doesn't want you thinking otherwise."

"I appreciate you running interference cousin. It's good that you said something."

"Can I tell her you said that?"

"Sure, I hope that relieves her concerns."

"I'm sure it will. You do realize her parents are King Cepheus and Queen Cassiopeia of Ætheopia, right?"

"Huh? What are you getting me into?"

"Do you like her?"

"Yes"

"You'll get used to it."

"Oh my god!"

"Yes, son?"

"Just saying, father."

Zeus and Achilles laughed at Persaeus who could do nothing but smile. He really couldn't say much as he knew this part of his life was going down a timeline that Zeus had already seen, and Persæus was not opposed to it. He would just have to travel it and see how it worked out. He really did like Andy and not just because she was extraordinarily beautiful. He was actually excited to meet her parents. Life was good and he was ready to face it head on.

The End

Made in the USA
Columbia, SC
04 July 2024

69b0f0e2-a432-47d8-abc7-4967e2f5692dR01